TUNES OF GLORY

for
G.St.Q.

James Kennaway (1928–68), was born in Aucherarder,
Perthshire, where he came from a quiet, middle-class
background and went to public school at Trinity College,
Glenalmond. When he was called to National Service in
1946 he joined the Queen's Own Cameron Highlanders
and served with the Gordon Highlanders on the Rhine.
Two years later he went to Trinity College, Oxford, where
he took a degree in economics and politics before renewing
his ambitions as a writer and working for a publisher in
London. Kennaway married his wife Susan in 1951, and
something of their turbulent relationship and his own
wild, charming, hard drinking and intense personality can
be found in *The Kennaway Papers* (1981), a book put
together by Susan after his death.

Tunes of Glory (1956), was Kennaway's first novel. It
remains his best-known work, and the author himself
wrote the screenplay for what was to become a hugely
successful film in 1960. His next book, *Household Ghosts*
(1961), was equally powerful. Set in Scotland as a tale of
family tension and emotional strife it was adapted for the
stage and then filmed – again to the author's own
screenplay – as *Country Dance* (1969). *The Bells of
Shoreditch* and *The Mind Benders* (also filmed), followed in
1963, while *Some Gorgeous Accident* (1967), and *The Cost
of Living Like This* (1969), develop Kennaway's restless
involvement with unhappy personal relationships and
love triangles.

At the age of only forty, James Kennaway suffered a
massive heart attack and died in a car crash just before
Christmas in 1968. A late novel *Silence*, was published in
1972.

James Kennaway

TUNES OF GLORY

Introduced by Allan Massie

CANONGATE
Edinburgh · London

First published in 1933 in Canada by Lester & Orpen Dennys Ltd

First published in Great Britain in 1956 by Putnam & Co Ltd

First published as a Canongate Classic in 1988
by Canongate Books Ltd,
14 High Street, Edinburgh, EH1 1TE

Copyright © M. St. J. H. Kennaway, 1956
Introduction copyright © Allan Massie, 1989

The publishers gratefully acknowledge general
subsidy from the Scottish Arts Council towards
the Canongate Classics series and a specific
grant towards the publication of this title

British Library Cataloguing-in-Publication Data
A catalogue record for this book is available on
request from the British Library

ISBN 978 0 86241 223 4

Typeset by Hewet Text UK Ltd, Edinburgh

Printed and bound in Great Britain by Clays Ltd, Elcograf S.p.A.

www.canongate.tv

Contents

Introduction

Tunes of Glory was James Kennaway's first novel, and has remained his most popular. It was published in 1956 to a chorus of critical approval. Evelyn Waugh wrote that Kennaway 'demonstrated a powerful natural talent which may well develop into something important'; Peter Quennell forecast that he 'would take his place amongst the finest story-tellers of the day'; Compton Mackenzie selected the novel as his Book of the Year.

It was filmed in 1960. Alec Guinness starred with John Mills, Dennis Price and Susannah York. There were smaller parts for Duncan Macrae, Gordon Jackson and John Fraser. The director was Ronald Neame; Kennaway himself wrote the script and was nominated for an Academy Award, few better films have been made so faithfully from a novel, and it is hard now to read the book without visualizing these actors and hearing their voices.

This is testimony not only to the merits of the film, but to the peculiar qualities of the novel; it is perhaps also an indication of something lacking in it. The writing is intensely cinematic. From the opening we are invited to use our eyes:

> there is a high wall that surrounds Campbell Barracks, and in the winter there is often a layer of crusted snow on top of it. No civilian rightly knows what happens behind that grey wall but everybody is always curious, and people were more than ever curious one January a year or two ago.

That first paragraph offers another invitation: to enter a closed, exclusive community. Kennaway speaks in the knowing tones of the insider; the young writer has a clubman's assurance, while the word 'crusted' applies to more than the snow. It hints at the nature of the community within the wall, and suggests that Kennaway is about to lift its lid for our enlightenment and enjoyment.

The knowing tone was not a pose, or not wholly. Kennaway was indeed an insider, though he was also conscious, for a number of reasons, of never entirely belonging. He was twenty-eight when the book was published, and his education had been that of a conventional member of the upper-middle classes. His father, a hero of the First War, was a writer to the signet, and the factor for a number of Perthshire estates; he was a wealthy man as a result of his part in various land sales, which included the deal by which part of the Gleneagles estate was sold to the LMS Railway Company for the famous hotel, and he sat on the board of a number of Scottish companies. James was educated at Trinity College, Glenalmond, and then, after National Service, during which he was commissioned into the Cameron Highlanders before serving with the 1st Battalion the Gordon Highlanders in Occupied Germany. Thereafter, he went to Trinity College, Oxford. He was successful at every stage of his education, never in any sense a rebel.

Yet his self-assurance was perhaps less than it appeared. His father had died when James was twelve, and the boy had had to assume family responsibilities prematurely; he was acutely conscious of his duty towards his mother. He felt a compulsion to excel, if only to prove that he had not been diminished by his father's death. Moreover, he was sensitive about his social position: a factor's membership of the upper class was conditional, not absolute. The young Kennaway felt himself to be a member of an exclusive club, but one who could easily be displaced.

His attitude to the Army was similarly ambivalent. He enjoyed the experience of being an officer, and revelled in life as a privileged member of the occupying force in post-war Germany; but he disliked his regiment, finding in the Gordons 'a pettiness and filth which is hard to believe'. The batallion was troubled by internal rivalries: according to his biographer Trevor Royle, the regiment in *Tunes of Glory* 'is

undeniably the Gordons and most of the characters are based
on officers he knew in Germany'. He was offered a regular
commission, but declined, very nearly (or so he confided to
his mother) telling the Colonel 'that I would rather serve in
the Argentine Police than in his regiment'.

He went up to Oxford to read PPE (Politics, Philosophy
and Economics) with the eventual intention of becoming a
barrister. This was abandoned when he fell in love with
Susan Edmonds. This love affair dominated his last year
there, and they were married a few months after he came
down. Otherwise he had dabbled in Conservative politics (he
used to dream frequently of Winston Churchill) and in the
theatre; he had enjoyed social life, with the help of a private
income; he had not worked, and his degree was a poor one.
He joined a publishing firm, but he already believed that
his true metier was writing. In the next few years he
published a few short stories, before *Tunes of Glory* justified
that belief.

Tunes of Glory is a dramatic novel. It is the story of the clash
of opposites, and it is simple enough to be outlined in a
paragraph. Jock Sinclair, the Acting Colonel of the regiment
—ex-ranker and war hero, a rough swaggerer who came into
the army by way of Barlinnie Jail and the Pipe Band—is
superseded by Basil Barrow, Eton and Sandhurst, a product
of the Staff College, a gentleman, everything Jock is not.
Both are more complicated than they seem, men of action
who live on their nerves. Jock drinking too much, is haunted
by the ghosts of the past; Barrow by memories of his failed
marriage and his terrible years in a Japanese P.O.W. camp.
Naturally they clash; naturally the Officers' Mess is split.
Then Jock blunders: he strikes a corporal, unknown to him,
is his daughter's boyfriend, and he does so in the public bar of
a hotel in the town. He has played into Barrow's hands, but
Barrow does not know how to play the cards he has been
dealt. For a moment it seems as if Jock will crack first, but he
pulls himself together and rebuffs Barrow's conciliatory
overtures with contempt. Meanwhile Barrow tries to evade
the responsibility for deciding what should be done. He

consults Jock's closest friend, Major Charlie Scott, who refuses however to give him the answer he clearly seeks. Jock, Scott says, has to pay for what he's done: 'you can't have chaps striking corporals'. Faced with this respsonsibility, and crushed by his inability to rise to it, Barrow escapes in the only way open to him: he shoots himself. Jock's shame and pity are roused. He decrees for Barrow a military funeral on a scale more suitable for a Field-Marshal. At the end of giving his instructions for the funeral, he suffers a nervous and moral collapse.

The ending, not entirely convincing in the novel, works more effectively in the cinema where visual images, music and Guinness's presence supplement the words. Despite this reservation, *Tunes of Glory* is a strikingly competent first novel and I use the adjective in no derogatory sense: competence in fiction is sufficiently rare to call forth admiration.

It is a story of men within an institution. The women— there are only two, Jock's daughter Morag, and Mary Titterington, an actress at the locak Reportory theatre, sometimes Jock's mistress, and sometimes Charlie Scott's— receive short shrift. These are men who define themselves by their relationship to the regiment. Kennaway's understanding of this is both subtle and penetrating: Charlie Scott betrays Jock, and no doubt sexual jealousy has a part to play in this betrayal; but it is not the most important element. Jock realizes this himself: 'Charlie's a good soldier'. Within the terms according to which they have contracted to live their lives, and to be judged, Charlie is right enough. He might say to Jock what Muriel Spark's Sandy Stranger said to Jean Brodie: "if you did not betray us it is impossible that you could have been betrayed by us. The word betrayal does not apply." Jock's act of folly is itself a betrayal of all that the military code represents; it threatens to destroy the respect for hierarchy which makes the institution function.

Kennaway understands this, and shows that Charlie Scott is justified within the terms of *la vie militaire*. I put that in French, not as a flourish, but in the hope that the French phrase will suggest that this novel—and Charlie Scott's betrayal—would be more comprehensible to continental nations that have made a cult of the Army than they have been to most English critics.

Nevertheless these critics have a point too, and Kennaway sympathizes with them. He lets us see that other standards of judgement are possible, that indeed the code by which the regiment lives is in some way defective: it excludes the humane virtues, it denies imaginative understanding. Such exclusion and such denial breaks Barrow; the recognition that sympathy and imagination have their value breaks Jock in his turn.

Kennaway is a moralist and an ironist; there is judgement even in his descriptive prose. Throughout his fiction he is intensely concerned to place his characters, and he does so in order to evaluate them. His writing is exact, lapidary, appraising; he belongs to a Scottish tradition at the head of which stands Stevenson. He resembles Stevenson in another characteristic too; both writers are able to see virtue in energy, to extend their sympathies to characters very unlike themselves, men who swagger and act by instinct. Stevenson offers us Alan Breck Stewart, and Kennaway answers with Jock Sinclair. He is, I think, an equally remarkable creation.

There is a sense in which *Tunes of Glory* had no successor. Peter Quennell had suggested that Kennaway would become 'one of the finest story-tellers of his time'. He didn't not. Though he never neglected narrative, and was always aware of its importance, he moved away from the straightforward style of which he had shown himself a master in his first book. He experimented with the indirect approach, seeking to explore the complexity of human beings by varying the angle from which he viewed them. Indeed, he came to dislike *Tunes of Glory*: it had been too easy, it was a novel which had been 'given to him', which he had not been obliged to quarry. This was natural. Just as a mother may favour the child who has given her most trouble, so an author may set most value on the book which has caused him the greatest difficulty. It does not mean however that it is his best.

In fact, though Kennaway was to write novels which treated individuals in society with more subtlety and discri-

mination, *Tunes of Glory* has remained his most popular
work. There is good reason for this: he achieved here a
perfect marriage of matter and manner. It is not however
quite true to say that it had no successor. In his last work, the
posthumously-published novella, *Silence*, he recaptured the
rapidity which he had displayed in his first novel. That little
book is remarkable; intense drama contained within pure
narrative.

It was a tragedy for literature that he died, at the age of
forty, just when he had succeeded in bringing the two sides of
his talent together in the most complex and ironical work he
had yet achieved.

Allan Massie

BOOK ONE

The Complexion of the Colonel

There is a high wall that surrounds Campbell Barracks, and in the winter there is often a layer of crusted snow on top of it. No civilian rightly knows what happens behind that grey wall but everybody is always curious, and people were more than ever curious one January a year or two ago.

The north wind had blown most of the snow to the side of the barrack square, and not a soul walked there; not a canteen cat. In the guardroom the corporal commanding the picket was warming his fingers on a mug of hot tea, and the metalwork on the sentry's rifle was sticky with frost. In the bathhouse the Battalion plumber was using a blow-lamp on the pipes, and he had reached the stage of swearing with enjoyment. The sergeants were in their Mess, singing to keep themselves warm, and drinking to keep themselves singing. National Servicemen wished they were home in their villas, and horn-nailed Regulars talked of Suez; even the bandboys wished they were back at borstal. In the Married Quarters, the Regimental Sergeant-Major, Mr Riddick, was sandwiched between his fire and his television set.

But it was warm in the Officers' Mess. Dinner was over, and the Queen had had her due. The long dining-room with the low ceiling was thick with tobacco smoke. The regimental silver cups, bowls and goblets shone in the blaze of the lights above the table, and from the shadows past colonels, portrayed in black and white, looked down at the table with glassy eyes. Two pipers, splendid in their scarlet, marched round and round the table playing the tunes of glory. The noise of the music was deafening, but on a dinner night this was to be expected.

The officers who owned 'Number Ones' were in their blue tunics and tartan trews. Sitting back from the table they crossed their legs and admired their thighs and calves.

They moved their feet and felt the comfort of the leather Wellingtons that fitted closely to the ankle. Only one or two of the subalterns who could not rise to Number Ones were wearing khaki tunics and kilts. But, drunk to the stage of excited physical consciousness, they too crossed their legs and glanced with anxious pride at their knees. They had folded their stockings to make the most of the muscles of their legs, and they wore nothing under their kilts. Some were anxious that the dinner should finish early giving them time to visit their women. Others of a more philosophic turn of mind had resigned themselves by now. They had ruled out the idea of visiting a woman and they were now falling into a slow stupor. Both sets of officers would in the end return to their bunks, thoroughly dispirited, and breathless with the cold of three o'clock in the morning. The lover as likely as not, if he were still a subaltern, would be disappointed to the point of pain, and the philosopher, bowing patiently and bowing low to the inevitable, would be sick. And both would live to fight another day.

But it was at this point in the evening, when the pipers played, that the officers could see most clearly how the night would end. Their fate lay in the hands of the man sitting half way up the table, and in spite of the Mess President at the head, nobody could deny that the table was commanded by the unforgettable figure of Acting Lieutenant-Colonel Jock Sinclair, D.S.O. (and bar).

The Colonel's face was big and smooth and red and thick. He had blue eyes—they were a little bloodshot now—and his voice was a sergeant's. His hair, which was thin, was brushed straight back with brilliantine. It was not a bit grey. The Colonel did not look broad because he was also deep, and had the buttons on his tunic been fastened there would have been little creases running across his chest and stomach. But at times such as this he was inclined to unfasten his buttons. He had even unfastened the top two buttons of his trews this evening and his striped shirt protruded through the gap in the tartan. His trews were skin tight and it looked as if he need only brace his muscles to tear the seams apart. In his lap he nursed a very large tumbler of whisky, and he tapped his foot on the ground as the pipers played. He did not seem to find the music too loud.

From time to time he glanced round the table, and other officers when they caught his eye quickly turned away while he continued to stare. The look in his eye was as flat as the sole of his polished boot.

He had already made the pipers play three extra tunes that night, and as they played *The Green Hills* for the second time he hummed, and the music comforted him. He put his glass on the table when the room was silent again.

'Get away with you,' he said, surprisingly kindly, to the Corporal-Piper and as the pipers marched out of the room the officers applauded in their usual way: they banged their fists on the table and stamped their feet on the floor-boards. Jock sent orders that the pipers should be given double whiskies, then he leant back in his chair and groaned, while his officers talked. It was some minutes later when one of the younger subalterns at the far end of the table caught his attention. Jock tipped forward in his seat and put his clenched fists on the table. The flat eye grew narrow; the meat on his face quivered, and along the table conversation died on the lips. He made a suppressed sound which was still something of a shout:

'MacKinnon, boy!' Then he lowered his voice to a hiss. 'For Christ's sake smoke your cigarette like a man. Stop puffing at it like a bloody debutante.' He moved his hand as though he were chucking away a pebble, and he spoke loudly again. 'Get on with you; smoke, laddie, smoke . . .'

There was silence in the room as the young subaltern put his cigarette to his lips. He held it rather stiffly between two fingers and he half closed his eyes as he drew in the tobacco smoke. There was still a hush. He looked nervously at his Colonel as he took the cigarette from his lips. Even the movement of his wrist as he brought the cigarette down to the plate had something inescapably feminine about it, and this made Jock shake his fist. The boy's mouth was now full of smoke and he sat very still, with his eyes wide open.

'Go on then, laddie; draw it in, draw it in.'

MacKinnon took a deep breath which made him feel a little dizzy and he was glad that the Colonel could not resist a

joke at this point. The sound of his little cough was drowned
by the laughter that greeted his Colonel's witticism. Jock
looked from side to side.

'We've got laddies that've never put it in, I know,' he said
with both a wink and a nod. 'What I didn't know is how
we've one who can't even draw it in, eh?' When he laughed
the veins on his temple stood out. Then the laugh, as usual,
deteriorated into a thick cough, and he shook backwards and
forwards in an attempt to control it.

The officers were a mixed collection. One or two of them,
such as Major Macmillan, who was perpetually sunburnt,
seemed very much gentlemen, although they too laughed at
Jock's jokes. The others, if not gentlemen, were Scotsmen.
The younger they were the larger were their jaws, the older they were the fatter were their necks, except of course
for the Quartermaster, Dusty Millar, who had no neck at
all.

At last Jock recovered himself. 'Aye,' he said, with a final
cough, 'aye . . . Well gentlemen, I have news for you.'

Someone at the far end of the table was still talking.

'All of you, you ignorant men.' Jock raised his voice. 'News
that'll affect you all.' He paused. 'Tomorrow there's a new
colonel coming, and he'll be taking over the Battalion. D'you
hear? D'you hear me now?'

All the officers hesitated. Their jaws dropped and they
leant forward to look at Jock, who was looking at his tumbler.

Macmillan had a light-comedy voice. He touched his fair
hair with his hand and he said, 'Come, Jock, you're pulling
our legs.'

'Aye,' someone said uncertainly, disbelievingly. 'That's
it, isn't it?'

'What I'm telling you is true.' Jock took a sip of his drink.
'Ask Jimmy Cairns. Jimmy knows right enough.'

Cairns, who was his Adjutant, did not know what to say
but felt it was a time when something should be said. He
moved his hands, and he frowned.

'That's the way of it,' he said.

'Och . . .' The Quartermaster moaned, and others echoed
him.

'That's not right,' one said; and another, 'It can't be true.' The Battalion without Jock as C.O. seemed then an impossibility.

Jock raised his hand in the smoky air.

'We didn't ask for comments,' he said. Then, glancing at the younger officers at the far end of the table, some of whom did not seem so dismayed by the news, he added, 'One way or the other,' and he showed his teeth when he grinned. He grew solemn again and drew his hand down his face and wagged his head, as if to clear his vision. 'It's just a fact,' he said slowly, 'it's just a fact,' and he leant back in his chair again.

Major Charlie Scott, who sat next to Jock, had an after-dinner habit of stroking his large red moustache, but he dropped his hand to ask, 'What's his name, eh?'

'Basil Barrow.'

'Major Barrow?' a clear-voiced subaltern said at once. 'He lectured at Sandhurst. He's an expert on Special . . .' Suddenly aware that he had sounded a little too enthusiastic, his voice trailed away. He looked around, brushed some ash from his trews, and continued in a nonchalant tone, 'Oh, he's really quite all right; they say he's frightfully bright upstairs.' The officers looked towards the Colonel again. They were gradually recovering.

'Aye,' Jock said. 'He went to Oxford, if that means any-thing. They say he was a great success as a lecturer or what-ever he was. Quite a turn with the cadets.' He gave a mali-cious grin and another big wink. Then he belched and made a sour face. He took another drink of whisky.

'Colonel Barrow's a man about forty-four. Eton—aye, it's right, what I'm telling you—Eton and Oxford. He joined the Regiment in 1935 and he was only with it a year or two before being posted on special duties. He has some lan-guages, so it seems. It's as young Simpson says. He's bright upstairs. He got the M.C. and he was taken prisoner pretty early on.' Jock swung his eyes around the table. 'I know all about him; you see that?'

'There was a fellow we used to call Barrow Boy. D'you remember him? A lightweight chap; good at fencing, if I recall.'

'I remember. Good Lord, yes.'

Jock spoke again. 'That's the same chum. That's him. He was well placed in the Pentathlon sometime just before the war.' He grew suddenly tired of the subject. 'Well, he's to command the Battalion and I'll have another tumbler of whisky.'

A Mess steward dashed forward and replaced the empty glass with a full one. On nights like this Jock's drinks were lined up on a shelf just inside the pantry door; lined up in close formation.

'And what about you, Jock?' Cairns asked.

'Aye. And what about me, china?'

'You staying on?'

'Unless you're going to get rid of me, Jimmy.'

Cairns knew just how far he could go with Jock.

'I thought there might be a chance of it.'

Jock was about to smile when the same subaltern who had known Barrow interrupted. 'Staying on as second-in-command, you mean?' and he was too young and a little too well spoken to get away with it. His seniors glanced immediately at the Colonel. Jock eyed the boy with real hatred, and there was a very long pause.

One of the stewards by the pantry door all but dropped his salver; his eyes grew wide, and he felt the hair rising at the back of his neck. Goblets and glasses poised in the air, whisky stayed in the mouth, unswallowed, and the swirly cloud of smoke above Jock's head for one instant seemed perfectly still.

Jock spoke very sourly, and quietly. 'So may it please you, Mr Simpson,' was what he said, looking back to his tumbler.

'Oh, I'm glad you're not leaving us, sir.' But the answer came too glibly. Jock shrugged and gave a little snigger. He spoke as if he did not care whether he was heard. 'You're away off net, laddie . . . and, Mr Simpson?'

It was fairly easy to see that Mr Simpson had been a prefect at school. He looked the Colonel straight in the eye and he never quite closed his mouth.

'Yes, sir?'

'No "Sirs" in the Mess. Christian names in the Mess

except for me and I'm "Colonel". I call you just what I feel like. O.K.?'

'Yes, Colonel.'

'Yes, Colonel . . . Now, gentlemen; now then. This is Jock's last supper and there'll be a round of drinks on me. Even one for Mr Simpson. Corporal!'

'Sir.'

'Whisky. For the gentlemen that like it and for the gentlemen who don't like it, whisky.'

He turned apologetically to Charlie Scott, who was still stroking his moustache.

'I'm no good at talking at the best of times, Charlie, and tonight I'm no coping at all. Will we have the pipers back? It fills the gaps.'

'Whatever you say, Jock; it's your night.'

'Aye.' Jock opened his eyes very wide: this was one of his mannerisms. 'Aye,' he used to say, then with his eyes wide open he would add a little affirmative noise. It was an open-mouthed 'mm'. Aye, and a-huh. 'Well I say we'll have the pipers.' He leant back in his chair and addressed one of the stewards who was hurrying by with a bottle. 'Laddie, call the pipers.'

'This minute, sir.'

'Just "Sir".' He made a gesture with his flat hand: a little steadying gesture. It was the same gesture that had steadied men in the desert, in Italy, France, Germany and Palestine. 'Just "Sir". That's all you need say.' Then he sighed, and he said, 'Aye, Charlie.' He dug the point of his knife into the table-cloth again and again as he talked. He first made a hole with the knife and gradually he widened it.

'. . . And you'll have a tune, and I'll have a tune, and Macmillan here'll have a tune, and I'll have another tune. Charlie, why the hell d'you grow that moustache so big?'

Major Charlie Scott continued to stroke it with his fingers. His great green eyes grew wide, under the shepherd's eyebrows. He could think of no explanation.

'Dunno; I'm sure. Just grew.'

Jock leant his chair back on two legs again and his arms fell down by his sides. 'And you're not the great talker yourself.'

' 'Fraid not.'

'No . . . Well, let's have the music. *Ho-ro, my Nut Brown Maiden* for me, and for you, Charlie?'

'*The Cock o' the North.*' Jock tipped forward at that. The legs of the chair creaked as they pitched on the floor again.

'Yon's the Gordons' tune!'

'I still like it.'

Jock screwed up his face: he was genuinely worried.

'But yon's a cheesy tune, Charlie.'

Charlie Scott shrugged.

Jock leant forward to persuade him. 'Laddie, I was with them for a wee while. They didn't like me, you know; no. And Jock didn't care much for them, neither.'

'Really?'

'Can you no think of a better tune?'

'Myself, I like *The Cock o' the North.*' Charlie Scott put another cigarette in his holder.

Jock laughed and the veins stood out again. He slapped his thigh and that made a big noise.

'And I love you, Charlie; you're a lovely man. You're no a great talker, right enough. But you've a mind of your own . . . Aye, pipers, and where have you been?'

'Pantry, sir.'

'Are you sober?'

'Sir.'

'You'd bloody well better be, and that's a fact. You're no here to get sick drunk the same as the rest of us are.'

The drones began as the bladders filled with air. The pipers marched round and round again. The room grew smokier, and the officers sat close into their chairs as the drink began to flow. The stewards never rested.

TWO

The pipers were in the pantry, recovering themselves. They were drinking beer, and the sweat poured down their faces. Their heavy kilts and tunics were hot and scratchy, and all the paraphernalia of their dirks and plaids was a nuisance to them.

The younger piper had yellow eyes and he spoke in a high-pitched voice.

'He's a bloody terror, and that's what he is.'

'Aye,' said the Corporal, 'and he's a great man.'

'He's a bloody terror, and that's what he is; I'm telling you, Corporal.'

'You can close your mouth. You'll need all your spittle the night.'

Mess stewards in their white bum-freezers hurried by in search of liquor.

'Is it right he was a piper; is that right, Corporal Fraser?'

'Aye. And he could be Pipe-Major if he felt like it, man. You should hear him on the pibrochs. There's nobody to touch him. He's played on the wireless, you know.'

'I'm no a corporal; I never get the chance of listening to the bloody wireless.'

'You'll watch your language in the Officers' Mess, Piper Adam.'

'This is no the Officers' Mess. This is the pantry.' All around them were dirty plates and cutlery. 'Look at the shambles, eh?'

'Just the same.'

'Och, away you go, Corporal . . . He's a bloody terror; I'm telling you.'

'Aye, aye. You're telling me.'

The Corporal-Piper was a patient young man with the mild blue eyes of the far north. He came from that queer strip of

flat land called the Lairg. It stretches for thirty or forty miles
along the south side of the Moray Firth, and at no point is
it more than a few miles wide. The road from Inverness to
Fochabers is as straight as the pines trees there, and nowhere
in Scotland is there so much sky. It is like a foreign land,
and the people speak their English slowly, and with a mild
intonation, as if they were translating from a foreign tongue.
So it was with Corporal Fraser.

'Aye,' he said softly; and he finished his pint of beer.

Then they were called into the ante-room to play some
reels. Jock had decided that they all ought to take some exercise before the next round of drinks and as it was too slippery
for a race round the barrack square he ordered that there
should be dancing. With Charlie Scott as his partner he led
away with the 'Duke of Perth' while the others, standing in
their lines, clapped their hands to the music.

Jock danced with energy and with precision. He leapt high
in the air and landed miraculously softly on the toes of his
small feet. That was how he had been taught to dance and
the others had to try and dance like him. They put their
hands above their heads; they swung; they yelled; they
hooched. Then they had a drink and they began all over again
with a new dance. By this time they were very warm and many
of them had removed their tunics. Every officer in the Mess
was dancing amongst the pillars in the long ante-room when
the door opened and the new Colonel walked in.

For a moment, nobody observed him, and the dance continued. He was wearing a tweed suit and his jacket hung
open. He had a moustache and his hair was growing grey,
not at the temples where men like their hair to grow grey, but
all over. Round his large eyes there was a yellowish shadow
of tiredness, and his brow was lined. If you saw this man on
a platform at a railway station you would at once be certain
that there was a gun-case with his luggage; and you would
be right. There must be fifty colonels who look very much
like this one. He now stood quite still, as only an actor or a
soldier can. His hands rested by his sides.

Mr Simpson followed Piper Adam's eye, and he was the
first to recognise the stranger. He immediately moved up the
line to talk to Jock, who was absorbed with the dancing. He

tugged at his elbow. His voice had the delighted urgency of
the first man with bad news.

'Colonel!'

'What is it, laddie? Get down to your proper place.'

'The Colonel's here.'

'You're drunk, laddie.'

'Colonel Barrow. He's at the door.'

Jock looked round and stared, first at Simpson and then at
the newcomer. Only a moment before he had been beaming
with joy. He had joked with Charlie Scott as they gradually
worked their way up the set to start their second turn. He
had given a little imitation of some of Major Macmillan's
worse affectations on the dance-floor. Macmillan was a very
smooth performer, and had Jock not been there he would
hardly have bothered to move his feet at all. Jock meant no
harm by his little demonstration. He was in good spirits. He
had forgotten everything but the dancing and the drinking,
and the music tingled in his veins. He liked to feel the floor
bouncing. But suddenly the dancers and the pipers seemed
to fade away from him, and he forgot them. He stopped clap-
ping his hands and they hung in mid-air. A look of real pain
crossed his face and he said in a whisper, 'But dammit, he's
no due till the morn!'

Then his hands fell to his tunic and he began to button it
up. He pulled in his stomach and bit his lip. He shouted at
the top of his voice for the dancing to stop. The dancers heard
but the pipers continued to play. When he shouted again they
too understood and with a drone they ceased. Everybody now
turned towards the figure at the door. Colonel Barrow did not
sound nervous, but a little tired.

'Good evening, gentlemen.' His voice was very light. 'My
name is Barrow.'

Nobody replied. They looked at him, stunned. Then Jock
strode down the middle of the room, his heels clicking on
the boards. The two sets of dancers at each side of the room
still stood in loose formation and they watched him come to
a formal halt two paces away from the Colonel.

'Jock Sinclair. Acting Colonel.'

'I've heard a great deal about you.' The Colonel spoke in
the same light voice; he spoke pleasantly but seriously and as

the two shook hands the officers readjusted their dress. They
shifted about, and looked nervously at each other. Somehow, they felt guilty. Major Scott and the company commanders were duly introduced but Jock said there were too many
bloody subalterns—all subalterns were bloody, all subalterns were damned—to attempt an introduction there and
then. Jock behaved as if it were a parade. He was like one of
those commanders you see photographed looking down and
talking earnestly to his Queen.

'And now, Colonel,' his voice was very serious. 'May we
have permission to resume the dance that was interrupted?'

The Colonel looked surprised. 'For heaven's sake . . . I'm
not here officially until tomorrow. You're in command.'

'Very well.' Jock instructed Corporal Fraser and the others to carry on. 'Charlie, we best break off.' He turned to
the Colonel again. 'You'll join us in a drink?'

'Thank you. Brandy and soda.'

Jock blinked, and he looked down at his successor. 'Not
a whisky?'

'Not a whisky.'

'We all drink whisky in this Battalion,' Jock said, heavily.

'Oh, yes,' Barrow smiled pleasantly. 'I remember that.
Whisky doesn't really agree with me. D'you think we could
adjourn to the far end of the room? I find it rather noisy
here.'

Jock looked over his shoulder at the pipers playing behind
them.

'Whatever you like,' he said and he never smiled once. As
they walked the length of the room he glanced slantwise at
the Colonel, but the Colonel was intent on the dancing.

Barrow put his hands in his coat pockets as he walked up
the room, and once or twice he moved them with a nervous
little jerk. He twitched his moustache. The officers stared
at him and they noticed the rather sprightly step. He sprang
on the balls of his feet, again with a sort of nervousness. His
tread was as light as his voice.

'This is my farewell party, you understand,' Jock said
when they sat down. 'There's not a carry-on like this every
night. Four and a half years is a long time to command a

battalion, and then. . . .' He did not finish the sentence, and Barrow did not finish it for him. He waited, and Jock felt clumsy. His hands clasped and unclasped: they lost their way.

'Where the hell's that bloody steward got to?' he asked, and Charlie Scott, for something to do, went to find him.

Jock tried to settle in his seat and he undid the buttons of his tunic and trews.

'Charlie's a good lad . . . Aye. They're all good men, except for some of the babies, and they'll be good men in their time; some of them, anyway.'

Again Barrow kept silent.

'Ah, well; you found your way here all right?'

'I have actually been here before.'

Jock raised his eyebrows; he was heavily polite.

'Aye? When was that?'

'I came as a subaltern.'

'From Sandhurst?' The question was asked with an air of innocent curiosity.

'From Oxford, as a matter of fact.'

Charlie had now rejoined them and the steward brought the tray of drinks.

'From Oxford? Fancy that . . . Aye. And where were you before that?'

'I was at school.'

Jock nodded. They were sitting on the leather settee by the dining-room door, and the dancing seemed far away.

'Harrow, was it?'

'No.'

'Oh . . . I see, I see.' Charlie Scott did not approve of Jock's questions but every time he tried to interrupt Jock just raised his voice. Otherwise his voice was pitched at an unnatural low.

'A-huh. . . . You came in that way; with an Oxford degree.'

The Colonel smiled. He was leaning right back in the seat, with his head tipped back.

'For what it was worth.'

Jock eyed him for a moment and he ran his tongue along his lower lip. Then he gave a little flick of his head: 'Well I came in the other way. By way of Sauchiehall Street, Barlinnie gaol, and the band. I was a boy piper.'

'It sounds a much better training,' the Colonel answered pleasantly, and Jock breathed heavily. Charlie took his first opportunity.

'You'll have another drink, Colonel?'

'Forgive me. I'm rather tired. I think I'll turn in after this one.'

'Are you no going to have a dance?' The flat eyes rested on him.

'If you'll forgive me,' the Colonel said again. 'I've had a long day.'

'You drove up?' Charlie asked.

'Hell of a journey.'

Charlie was sympathetic. 'Family and all?'

The Colonel looked down at his brandy. 'I have no family. I'm by myself.'

Charlie smiled. He felt required to say something. 'Then we won't have to cope with the Colonel's wife.'

But the Colonel did not smile. He paused and sipped his drink. He replied suddenly, 'I suppose there's that to it.'

Then, the dance over, Macmillan came to pay his respects. Macmillan very quickly pitched the conversation on to a higher social level: the shooting and the shooting set. He mentioned some names; some names of titled people; but he did not, of course, mention the title. The Colonel was very pleasant. He did not seem to remember any of these people very clearly. He did not have any names to give in exchange.

Jock's head was cocked on one side. He had had enough whisky to make him persistent. 'It'll be some time since you were with the Battalion, I'm thinking.'

'Yes, I feel quite a new boy. It's some time since I've been with any battalion. I've been sitting behind a desk for a year.'

Charlie screwed up his face with horror. 'Ghastly . . .'

Macmillan said, 'Too boring.' Then he went on: 'One of the boys said you were at Sandhurst.'

The Colonel looked him in the eye.

'That would be Simpson,' he said, and Jock was surprised.

'Aye. You're right, now. He's over there. And what was it you said you did before Sandhurst?'

'I don't think I did say.' The Colonel was still very patient.
'You didn't?'

Charlie Scott and Sandy Macmillan glanced at each other.
The Colonel ran the tip of his finger round the rim of his
glass.

'Like you, Sinclair, I was in gaol.'

'A P.O.W.?' Jock gave a little snigger. 'That's not quite
the same thing.'

'I think I would have preferred Barlinnie gaol.'

THREE

But it was after Barrow had left them that the drinking really began. All the tunics were loose again. Jock sat on the leather guard in front of the log fire and the smoke from his cigarette crawled up his cheek, over his flat blue eyes. The junior subaltern caught his attention again.

'Mackinnon? D'you know the words of the Lord's Prayer?'

'Yes, Colonel.'

'You do?' Jock's eyes were very bloodshot now. It showed when he rolled them. 'Then you're not so bloody ignorant as I thought you were.' He stared at the boy, who looked very pale and nervous. It was no secret that he had already retired once that evening to be sick.

'Poor wee laddie. Can you smoke yet?'

'I think so.'

'Poor laddie . . . Och.' Jock was restless. He moved now to an armchair and he dropped into it. 'Och, to hell with all this,' he said impatiently. 'Och, to hell with all this.' Major Charlie Scott was lying full length on the settee beside Jock's chair and Jock now leaned over towards him.

'Charlie boy, are you dead yet?'

'Cold. As cold as Flora Macdonald.'

'I can tell you, chum, there's some is colder than her.'

Charlie made no reply further than to let his heavy eyelids drop again and Jock turned to the group still hanging around the ante-room. His voice was a sergeant's again.

'Get away with you, you bairns and cheeldron; away to your holes and your chariots. You've drunk more than you or I can afford and you're the worst lot of bastards I've ever known. And Jimmy Cairns is the worst of the lot of you.'

'I'm too tired,' Cairns said. 'I'm too tired even to insult you.'

18

'Just try and I'll have you drummed out of the Battalion.'
Jock's energy was unlimited.

'I'm whacked.'

'Good night, Jimmy lad.'

'Aye, Jock.'

The Corporal brought a full bottle and the others went to
bed, leaving Charlie Scott on the couch, stretched out like
a walrus on his back, and Jock sitting in his chair with his
knees apart and his hands clasping the arms. They sat there,
quiet for a long time. It was Charlie who spoke at last.

'You know, Jock; I once had a woman under water.'

Jock hardly seemed to be listening. 'Aye, man? Was it
salt or fresh?'

Charlie sat up. He looked rather dazed.

'Flesh,' he said. 'All flesh.' But Jock did not smile.

'Charlie, have I been such a bad colonel; have I, man?'

Charlie took a long time to reply. He seemed to have difficulty in finding the right words.

'Never known a better,' he said with a sharp shake of his
head.

'Och, man. Stop your fibbing. I asked a civil question.'

'Honest to God, old boy. In the war . . .'

Jock shook his head and he said, ' "Old boy, old boy,
old boy." '

'You asked me and I tell you. For God's sake, chum . . .'

'D'you really think that, Charlie?'

Charlie seemed a little irritated by his questions. He
touched his moustache. 'Sure, sure.' He gave an apos-
trophied nod and a little belch. Then he lay down again
and there was another pause. Jock drew a circle on the
leather arm of the chair with his forefinger and he traced
it again and again. Then he said in a whisper,

'It's no fair, Charlie. It's no right after four years and
another six months on top o' that. It isn't . . . Och, but
he's here now and what a spry wee gent he is. I fancy the
wee man's got tabs in place of tits.'

'Beyond me, Jock. Give us the bottle will you? There's
a good chum.'

'Aye, and you look as though you need a drink. That
bloody growth must take it out of you. You look pale.

But you're a terror with the women, Charlie; there's no
denying it. You're a great big bloody white-faced stoat with
bushy eyebrows.'

Charlie did not hear him. He was having difficulty with
his drink.

'I say, old man. D'you think we could dispense with the
glasses. Is that on?'

'Aye. Never mind the glasses. If anyone has a right to get
fu' the night it's big Jock Sinclair and his friend Charlie
Scott. Did you hear him say that about the whisky? He
doesn't drink it, you know.'

'Poor chap.'

'Aye. That's so; the poor wee laddie.' Jock ran that
one round his tongue with a mouthful of whisky. Then he
chuckled. 'The poor wee laddie . . . the new boy, he called
himself; all in his mufti. . . .'

Jock sat musing and sniggering for a moment or two, then
his resolution seemed to strengthen and he picked himself to
his feet.

'He'd no bloody right blowing in here like that without
warning me or Jimmy first. That wasn't right at all. It was
bad form. That's what that was.' Then he clenched his fists.
'Whatever way you look at it,' he said, 'they've no right to
put him in above me. And it makes me angry, Charlie. It
makes me bloody angry.' Charlie did not reply and Jock continued to walk up and down. Then at last he returned to his
chair and he tapped the arm of it with his finger. His eyes
were narrowed, and perfectly still. He did not even remember to smoke.

After a while, Charlie sat up and handed him the bottle.
Then he rubbed his eyes with his long freckled fingers.

'We're not great talkers, Jock.' Jock was tipping back the
bottle, and more out of politeness than anything else Charlie
went on, 'Not great talkers at all.'

'We'll have the Corporal-Piper,' Jock said.

'That's it, my boy.'

'That's just what we'll do. And we'll listen to the music.'

He rose clumsily to his feet and he shouted from the door
leading into the dining-room. In a moment Corporal Fraser
was with them, and Jock had to begin all over again.

'Have you been asleep, Corporal Fraser?'

'No, sir. I have not been asleep. I have been waiting, sir,' the Corporal replied slowly.

'And cursing and binding and swearing . . . Och, man, I've been a piper mysel'.'

'Aye, sir.'

Jock looked up. 'And I was a bloody sight better than you.'

'Yes, sir.'

Jock paused; then he cocked his eyebrow and put his head on one side. 'Have you got a bint down town, Corporal? Have we kept you away from her, eh?'

The Corporal stood to attention. His cheeks had coloured a little.

'You've got a lassie, have you, eh? Well, Corporal, have you got a tongue in your head?'

'Aye, sir.'

'You've got a lassie?'

'Aye, sir.'

The Corporal looked more than uneasy; but Jock persisted.

'What d'you think of that, Charlie? The Corporal's got a lassie.'

'Good for the Corporal.'

'No, no, Major Scott, that's no the thing to say at all.' Jock looked at him very disapprovingly.

'No?'

'No. You should say "Good for the lassie!" Aye, and good for the lassie. It's not every lassie that catches a Corporal-Piper. No it's not. Is she bonny, Corporal?'

'I think so, sir.'

'"I think so," he says; d'you hear that? And, tell me Corporal,' Jock's voice was scarcely more than a whisper, 'Are your intentions strictly honourable?'

'Aye indeed, sir,' the Corporal said stoutly.

Now Jock raised his voice: 'Then you're a bloody foo', Corporal; that's what you are. You're far too young for that. A soldier shouldn't marry young. You leave honourable intentions to fathers like me. It's a father's worry, anyway. I always say if I catch my lassie at it, I'll welt the laddie, but I'll probably never catch her, anyway. So there we are. He's too young for honourable intentions, is he no, Charlie?'

Charlie nodded vigorously. 'I'm too young,' he said.

'You're a bloody rogue, Major Scott; that's what you are. No mistake.'

'Has the Corporal had a drink, Colonel?'

But the Corporal interrupted: 'No, thank you, sir. Not if I'm going to play, sir.'

'We didn't bring you here to look at your dial, however bonny the lassie may think it is. I can tell you that, Corporal. . . . We'll have a tune now. We'll have *Morag's Lament* again.' Jock looked solemnly at the Corporal. 'Morag was the name of my lassie, once upon a time, and Morag's the name of my wee girl.'

'Sir.'

'And then we'll have *The Big Spree*. After that we'll think and you'll have something to wet your lips. Come away with you then. Come away with you.'

To the unpractised ear a pibroch has no form and no melody, and to the accustomed ear it has little more. But it is a mood and a pibroch was something Jock felt almost physically; damp, penetrating and sad like a mist. It enveloped him and pulled at his heart. He was far too much the professional to be moved to tears, but the Corporal played well and it took a moment before Jock fully recovered himself. The pibroch very often comes to a sudden end; it is a finish that makes it a fragment, and the more sad for that. Jock nodded his head slowly, three times.

'Corporal Fraser, you'll make a piper yet.'

The Corporal gave a sunny smile.

'Aye, you're better at the pibroch than I'd known. Your grace-notes are slurred but otherwise it was good. Now give me the pipes, lad; we'll have a turn ourself.'

In his trews, with his fat bottom waggling as he marched up and down the room, Jock looked comic. To begin with, he looked comic. But soon he was in the full rhythm of the tune, and he was absurd no longer. A good piper is like a rider who is one with his horse, and Jock was soon part of the music. He played some marches, with a fault or two;

then a slow march; then a faultless pibroch. That is something that a man does only a few times in his life; and the Corporal was dumb with admiration.

As he slowly laid the pipes down, Jock himself was aglow with pride. He was sweating with the exertion, but his eyes too were glistening. He was like a schoolboy who has won his race.

'That's how to play the movement, laddie. It's no just a question of wobbling your fingers on grace-notes.'

The Corporal at last found his voice.

'I've never heard the pibroch better; never better.'

Jock nodded shyly.

'I don't think I've ever played it better. So there you are. You have to be in the mood for the pibroch; it is a lament. It is a lament.' He mopped his brow. 'But it is something else as well. That's the catch. It's no just a grieving. There's something angry about it too.' Charlie Scott was sure it was all beyond him and in a moment Jock said, 'Och, well, Corporal, you'll be wanting away to your lassie. You'll have to jump the wall.'

'It's too late for that now, sir.'

'D'you hear that, Charlie? The lassie'll have gone home to bed. Now see what you've done.'

'Wise woman.'

'Then away you go, Corporal. Away to your own bed.' The Corporal put on his bonnet and came sharply to attention.

'Permission to dismiss, sir.'

Jock looked up at him. He liked the formality. Suddenly he approved of the Corporal.

'D'you want me to help you with that pibroch, Corporal?'

'Very much, sir.'

Jock nodded. 'A-huh,' he said, and he clasped his hands and bent forward in his chair. 'Tomorrow morning?'

Charlie said, 'You'll be in no sort of shape tomorrow morning.' But Jock ignored him.

'Half-past twelve?'

'I'll be in the gym then, sir.'

'What are you up to in the gym?'

'Boxing, sir.'

'You're a boxer? Light-heavy, is it?'

'That's it, sir.'

'Then we'll meet some other time. You're a man after my heart, Corporal. We'll make a piper of you yet.'

'Thank you, sir.'

Jock nodded again. He made a little gesture. 'Dismiss.'

Through the biting cold, the Corporal made his way back to his bunk in the band's quarters. He was shivering in spite of the whisky inside him, when, half undressed, he slipped between the rough blankets and drew his greatcoat over the bed. He had put newspapers between the blankets earlier in the evening, and now he was glad of them. As he lay there he could see the cloud of his breath in the pale light of the barrack lamp which shone through the narrow window by his head, and he felt a soldier's loneliness. He thought for a moment of the grace-notes, and the pibroch; then he thought of his girl; just thought of what she looked like. He wished he could keep her more constantly in his mind but she kept slipping away from him, and away again as he slowly fell asleep. But in his dreams her face was transformed, for the Corporal dreamt of his Colonel.

The bottle was three-quarters empty.

'You're a miserable man,' Charlie said. 'It's not three-quarters empty. It's a quarter full.'

'It's your turn.'

'I had some when you were blowing your guts out.'

'You have no music in you. No music in you at all.'

Jock put the bottle to his lips again, then he held it in his lap. The chairs all round faced one way and another. It was as if a storm had abandoned them there.

'I was thinking as I played, Charlie. I should have been the Pipe-Major; that's what I should have been. But that was not the way of it. And I've acted Colonel, and I bloody well should have been Colonel, and by this hand boy, I bloody well will be Colonel. I will.'

But Charlie was snoring. For an instant Jock looked as if he were going to kick him, then he seemed to see the joke.

'Oh, you bastard,' he said slowly and gently. He pronounced the word with a short *a*. 'Oh, you bastard!

You're no a good listener, either.' And alone he finished the bottle.

Like a bath of water, the room grew slowly colder and Jock sat dazed. He could not bring himself to move, though the hand which clasped the empty bottle grew icy cold. At last he bit his lip and, stiffly, rose to his feet. Then gently—and it took great strength—he lifted Charlie in his arms, and a little unsteadily, carried him upstairs. He placed him on his bed, and threw a couple of blankets over him. Charlie was still sound asleep. And Jock smiled on him, as if he were a child.

He brushed his hair in front of the mirror, and once more he buttoned his tunic and his trews. He lit a cigarette, and with great concentration he found his way to the cloakroom where he remembered to collect his bonnet and coat. The air outside made him gasp. The wind had dropped but the sky was starless; there would certainly be more snow before morning. He dug his heels into the ground in the approved fashion, but this did not prevent him slipping on the icy patches. Precariously, he picked his way round the barrack square. As he marched up to the gate he walked more confidently and he swung his arms. Then suddenly he felt an urge to call out the guard and he instructed the sentry to shout the necessary alarm. The guardroom came to life with the sound of swearing and of soldiers clambering off their steel bunks. Rifles were dropped and somebody kicked over a tin mug; knife, fork and spoon were scattered over the concrete floor. But by the time they had formed in their correct rank outside Jock seemed to have lost interest in the proceedings. He could see a fault in the dress of every man there but he did not bother to inspect the guard. He just returned the Corporal's salute, and without a word went on his way. He left the guard bewildered and the Corporal apprehensive.

FOUR

On such a night and at such a time he tended to call on Mary
Titterington, but it was six weeks now since he had seen
her and he had decided on the last occasion that he would
not call again. She worked with a local repertory company
and his association with her was one of the many things that
the town and county objected to. Not that that made any
difference to him.

Anyway, when he left the barracks he thought about calling on her and instead of returning home over the old footbridge he wandered into the town. She had a flat in one of the
big houses by the park. He turned his collar up, and he dug
his hands into his greatcoat pockets. He passed nobody and
the only sound was the echo of his own footsteps. All cities
are lonely at night, but the old Scottish ones are lonelier than
all. The ghosts wander through the narrow wynds and every
human is a stranger surrounded, followed, and still alone.
The ghosts always unnerved Jock. He was suddenly chilled
and very lonely, so he turned back and went straight home.

Safe inside, he was glad to find his daughter had waited up
for him; he let his shoulders drop, and he smiled kindly at
her when he said, 'Lassie, you should be tucked up in your
bed.'

'Och, I couldn't sleep.'

'It's late. It's awful late.'

'I know it is. It's two o'clock.'

'You should be getting your beauty sleep.'

'It'll take more than sleep to make me a thing of beauty,'
she said with efficient presbyterian modesty. She was really
quite pretty, with pink cheeks, even at two in the morning;
but Morag never gracefully accepted a compliment.

Their home was one of those little villas with bow windows
and a staircase that runs straight down to the front door.

26

There was an ugly overhead light in the cramped hall and there was no carpet, but brown linoleum on the floor. Morag was in a sensible woollen dressing-gown and fluffy bedroom slippers. She came downstairs to help him with his coat.

'You look all in,' she said.

'Aye, I'm tired.'

'Did you come straight home?'

Jock glanced at her. They never mentioned Mary Titterington and he was not even sure that Morag knew of her, or knew about her.

'Of course I came straight back. Where the hell d'you think I'd go?'

'I don't know, father, I'm sure. But you look tired.'

'A-huh.'

'Come on into the kitchen. There's a kettle on. I guessed you'd be all in.'

Jock touched her shoulder with his hand. 'You're a good lassie, Morag. That's what you are. I shouldn't leave you alone like this, so often.' He wanted to say more, but he paused and she spoke first.

'Heavens, Father! What's got into you? D'you think the bogey-men'll get me?' She moved away and his hand dropped to his side. She never allowed him to be demonstrative. She was far too sensible for scenes. Her mouth gave her character away. It was a very pretty mouth, neither too small nor too large. But it was firm, and her lips were always closed tightly together. She had a neat firm chin, a short nose, light brown eyes and dark hair which fell in an orderly little roll round her neck. She walked quickly into the kitchen and Jock followed slowly. He laid his coat on a chair, and later Morag would tidy it away.

'I passed a tinker woman in the street. That mad woman. She was wheeling her barrow. And at this time of night. It's a wonder they don't burn her. They burnt her mother for a witch.'

Morag tutted. 'You don't believe all that nonsense, do you? Her mother was never a witch.'

'She was the last witch. That's a fact.'

Morag smiled. 'Och, away you go, Father. You'd believe anything.'

Jock was a little nettled.

'She's a terrible-looking woman anyway, with all her scarves and rags. What d'you suppose she keeps in the barrow?'

'Just what she pinches off honest folk.'

Jock sat down by the kitchen table and he played with the spoon in the sugar-bowl.

'She's eerie. D'you suppose she's anywhere to sleep? Walking along, talking to herself. She gives me the creeps. Aye, she does. I passed her on the cobbled wynd.'

Morag filled the teapot. She smiled at her father again.

'Were you feared?'

Jock cocked his head. 'Of course I wasn't feared.'

'I believe you were: same as all the rest of the kiddies. Did she tell you your fortune?'

'Aye and maybe. I didn't rightly hear what she was saying. And I'm bloody glad I didn't.'

'I thought you were keeping your swear words fc: the barracks,' Morag said primly, and Jock sighed and apologized. She handed him his cup of tea and he thanked her again. She sat down by the table. She pulled her chair in, and her back was upright.

'Well,' she said at last. 'And what's he like?'

'Who?'

'Your new Colonel, of course.'

'How the hell did you know he was here?'

'A wee birdie told me.'

'Aye, someone told you. Who's been here, eh?' He sounded annoyed.

'Nobody's been here. It's written plain across your face. I thought the new Colonel might come in tonight.'

Jock was not altogether satisfied with the explanation. He never allowed her to ring the Mess and ask after him, when he was late. He said this was because he did not want any officer rung by his womenfolk, but there were other more practical reasons. If he went round to Mary's flat he usually said he was going to the Mess. The Mess after all was his club; and a club should be a refuge. But Morag could read him like a book.

'I didn't ring the Mess,' she said truthfully. 'You can check up yourself.'

'I never said you did.'

'Maybe. Well, tell us. What's he like?'

'He's a wee man,' Jock said and he started to sip his tea.
He sipped it like a farmer in from the fields, with both hands
on the cup and his eyes straight in front of him. He did not
want to talk about Barrow. Morag softened a little, and she
said in a low voice:

'Father, it had to be.'

'I just said he was a wee man.'

'It had to be.'

Jock put down his cup and he lit a cigarette, knowing as
he did so that he had smoked too many that day.

'As a matter of fact, I'm no with you. It need never have
been. But that's neither here nor there. It's my belief that
he'll no be C.O. for very long.'

'Father, you'll not do any stupid thing.' It was not a
question, but an instruction. She took the sugar-spoon away
from him. 'If he's any sense at all he'll no give you a second
chance. You must promise me you'll not do any stupid thing.'

'Are you feared, Morag?'

'Och, I know you. I know you fine, Father. What's his
name?'

'Barrow. Poor wee man.'

'You're bitter.'

'Och, for Pete's sake Morag: d'you expect me to give a
cheer? Ach. . . .' He returned to his tea-cup and they spoke
no more on the subject.

Morag listened, when she got back to bed, and it was a
long time before Jock threw off one shoe, then the other. He
gave a great groan, and she heard the springs of the mattress
creak. Only then did she herself relax, but before she fell
asleep she heard Jock give an unusual sigh that was long and
trembling. After a moment's hesitation she knocked on the
wall.

'Are you warm enough? Have you got enough blankets?'

'You go to sleep or I'll skelp your bottom.'

And she tutted at his vulgarity.

FIVE

In the town, a week later, everybody was telling everybody how much milder it was. They were congratulating themselves on it, as if to say Scotland wasn't such a cold place as people made it out to be. They were delighted to hear that it had been bad weather in the South. They had letters from their sons and relations confirming it.

Behind the wall the detention squad was clearing away the last of the snow and the ice, and it was almost uncomfortably warm in the Officers' Mess after lunch. The stewards had cleared the last of the coffee-cups from the ante-room but the officers still did not move.

Superficially there was an air of extreme boredom. The company looked as sophisticated as a cavalry Mess. There was a whisper of glossy pages turning over and a flap as one magazine was exchanged for another. The officers were apparently sitting about wishing they had not tackled the treacle pudding, or promising themselves that they would stop drinking pinks before lunch. There was a smell of cigarette smoke and newsprint, and the sounds of a billiards game being played in the adjoining room. The Mess was a club.

But the officers at Campbell Barracks were deceptive. They were no longer a set of indolent gentlemen with courageous instincts. It is doubtful whether some were gentlemen at all—but then a Mess is renowned for taking on the complexion of its Colonel, and Jock had held command for some years now: this at least was the explanation the county favoured. Had they known better, they would have realized that Campbell Barracks was only one of the many that had suffered the same change. Whether or not it was a matter for regret, it was now an error to believe that the Regiment was commanded by asses. The billiards game

next door was not being played for a guinea or two. The
officers were not familiar with all the faces they saw in
these magazines. Nor were they bored. They were a set
of anxious and ambitious men, and some were extremely
shrewd. Indeed, the only thing they shared with their
fairy-tale forefathers on the walls was their vanity, and even
this took different forms. Sandy Macmillan was one of the
few whose vanity resembled the old set's. He wore his hair
a trifle longer than the regulations formally demanded, he
was a scratch golfer, he was never seen out of barracks in a
uniform and he wore dark glasses when he drove his sports
car. He was lying in one of the deepest chairs that afternoon
and his battledress was unbuttoned at the cuff. His stockings
were nearly white to make his brown knees look browner
and he hoped soon to be posted to Fontainebleau on some
United Nations lark. His vanities were not complicated, and
his income was largely private. He talked to Simpson, the
prefect, who had been attracted to him on arriving at the
barracks, and to young MacKinnon, the junior subaltern,
who had a face like a faun, and the manner of a gentleman.

The group in the next corner was not so obvious. The red-
haired Rattray, who was also christened Alexander, but who
styled himself Alec, had been educated at one of the Glasgow
day-schools, and he was a real pillar-box Scotsman. He was
aggressive in his masculinity and his nationality, and he was
busy growing a red moustache to be the more patriotic with.
He was violently ambitious and as near to stupid as any of the
subalterns reached; he insisted on seeing his face in the toe
of the boot of every man in his platoon. His only rival in strict
treatment of the men was his friend, Lieutenant Douglas
Jackson, who had a head like a German, a pasty complexion like a German, a fist like a German, and not unnaturally
an almost pathological hatred for Germans. Nothing nettled
him more than to be reminded that he had never actually
fought the Germans but had merely occupied their country
and seduced their young women.

There were as many other vanities as there were officers
in the room. Dusty Millar, the fat Quartermaster, had long
service and a couple of tricks with a matchbox for a shield;
Charlie Scott had his reputation; and the doctor had his

intellect. Perhaps the least vain of all was the Adjutant, Jimmy Cairns, a mature farmer's boy in uniform, completely and unaffectedly effective. Jimmy had a face to match his character. His expression was fresh and his hair was fair. He was growing, each year, more solid. But a second glance at him would have confirmed that the air of boredom was no more than superficial. He did not look happy now. He looked more worried than anyone, and he kept glancing at his watch.

Everybody looked up when Jock came in, and three or four dashed forward to tell him the bad news. He soothed them like children, like dogs. He put his palms out in front of him and waved them up and down in the air.

'For Jesus' sake,' he said, and apologized to the Padre who pretended he needed no apology. Then he got Cairns to tell him the story.

It had happened only half an hour before. After a week of tactful quiet, of asking questions and making no comments on the answers, of pointing here and nodding there, of listening and of inspection—after all this, the Colonel had made his first move, and he had made it when Jock was out of the Mess.

But telling the story, Cairns fell over himself to be fair.

The Colonel had ordered that the officers should forgather in the ante-room that afternoon at 1430 hours. He had put a notice on the board to that effect, just an hour before lunch. As they sat round disconsolately sipping their coffee, he blew into the ante-room, looking as light as thistledown. He was wearing his bonnet; and in the Mess. He asked them to sit in one corner of the room and as they assembled he stared out of the window at the low grey clouds. He seemed to be deep in thought, and far away from them. There was a minute before he recovered himself, and moving his walking-stick with his wrist he tapped the crook of it against his lips. Then he dropped it to the floor and addressed them in his sharp light voice.

'When I first came to this barracks the social responsibilities of an officer—and particularly of a subaltern— very greatly outweighed his military duties.' He glanced at Macmillan and Macmillan smiled, with a flash of white teeth, but the smile was not returned. The Colonel had not wasted his questions or his week. He knew their vanities too. 'This was quite common before the war. The last thing I want to do is re-establish that order.' The Quartermaster nodded 'hear, hear,' to that. He sank his chins into his chest and Barrow continued: 'We are first and foremost soldiers and the greater part of our energies must be devoted to training. On the range; drilling; marching; P.T. and so forth.'

They sat like a dull class. He cleared his throat and struck his stick against his thigh.

'On the other hand, gentlemen, it is necessary that we should play our full part in the social life of the locality. Very necessary. And for this reason it is important that we should maintain certain standards; standards which have been maintained for close on two hundred years. It is part of our responsibility.'

Nobody could guess what he was driving at, but nobody liked it. Some stared unblinkingly at the Colonel's face. Others shifted in their seats, raised their eyebrows and shrugged. The Colonel talked swiftly and without a trace of Scottish accent.

'Each Tuesday, Thursday and Saturday morning at 0715 hours all officers will report in this ante-room.' There was a mumble at that. '0715?' 'Saturday?' But Barrow did not seem to hear, and if he did hear, he did not heed. 'When the weather improves we may parade outside. For three-quarters of an hour there will be dancing, gentlemen. You will report dressed as you are now, but with plimsolls on, and the Adjutant will instruct the Pipe-Major to come and see me to make arrangements for a piper. All right?'

'Sir.' Jimmy sat up straight.

'The following dances will be mastered: the eightsome and foursome reels, the Duke of Perth, the Hamilton House, Duke and Duchess of Edinburgh, Petronella, the Cumberland Reel.'

'But, Colonel, the officers know these dances.' It was Rattray who spoke. It was a stupid thing to do, to interrupt at such a time, but his national dancing was a point of pride.

The Colonel's face remained blank, and the silence which
followed made even Rattray blush a little.

'No one,' the Colonel went on firmly, 'no one will raise
his hands above his head, except in the foursome reel. No
shouting, no swinging on one arm. We will go into these
details later. You will not be being trained for a professional
performance. You will be being—being reminded of the
manner of dancing traditionally adopted by an officer of this
Regiment.'

Cairns had intended to leave the story there, but everybody
was keen to tell what had happened next. Douglas Jackson
was something of a hero for what he had said next. At the
end of a long, hostile silence he had spoken clearly. Dusty
Millar was anxious that Jock should not miss this.

'Come on, Douglas, what did you say?'

Lieutenant Jackson had a deep voice to match his Prussian
head. 'I can't remember my words. I said I understood his
visit to the Mess that first night was quite unofficial. That's
the only time he's seen us dance.'

'Aye, that was it, that was it,' Dusty said, enjoying the
moment again.

Jock nodded. 'A-huh. And what did he say to that?'

'It *was* unofficial. That was all he said. But he was pretty
angry.'

The doctor grinned and sidled. 'Douglas is a marked man
now.'

Jock raised his eyebrows and he walked about, while they
waited. 'Well, well. I've always said some of the children
could do with a dancing class.'

'Och, heck,' Rattray said, flaming up. 'It's no dancing like
that we should be taught. We're not a lot of playboys.'

Jock opened his eyes wide. 'No.' He ran his tongue round
his cheek. 'No, we're not that.' Charlie knew the mood well:
he knew how much Jock was enjoying himself. He knew the
technique, and Charlie knew even before Jock turned that
he would walk away and touch one of the chairs with the
tips of his fingers.

'You notice he did it when you were out,' someone said.

'Maybe that was tact.' He spread out his hands. 'Gents,
we're no wanting any mutinies in this Battalion. We'll leave

that to the Navy.' Jock wagged his head. 'I think he's been very reasonable.'

Jimmy nodded. 'Of course he has.'

'Hell, this is the first thing he's done,' somebody said.

Jimmy smiled and tried again. 'There's bound to be some changes.'

'No one's denying that, Jimmy,' Alec Rattray said. 'But this is something different. The way we dance is our own business, isn't it? I'm no sure he's a Scotsman at all.'

'Aye,' they agreed.

'Dancing's off parade; and off parade's off parade.'

Macmillan suggested lightly, 'We do get a little rowdy.'

'Rowdy?' Jock turned on him. 'A-huh. You agree with the Colonel?'

'I'm not sure it was his business to . . .'

'You agree though: you agree?'

'By and large.'

'Aye,' Jock nodded. 'By and large. There you are then. It's what the doctor would call a difference of opinion, or emphasis or whatever the word is, down in Oxford. That's the way of it: so we best say no more about it. We don't want to be rent with schisms asunder. Do we?'

Jimmy had to leave then, and the others shifted places. They were not altogether satisfied, but had they known Jock as well as Charlie did, they would have realized that he had not finished. He was talking in his softest voice.

'It's always difficult, a change-over. It's as Jimmy says. Mind you, it seems a pity that he should choose the dancing. What time was this parade to be?'

Five or six voices replied: '0715.'

'Aye; and for the subalterns?'

A shout of 'No.'

'Oh, captains as well? . . . All officers? It's all officers, is it?'

'Aye, it is. That's what he said. Have you ever heard such bloody nonsense? Some of us have been dancing thirty years,' Dusty said hotly.

'Jock, we know you're in a difficult position . . .'

'I am: I am.' He shook his head seriously at that, but they gathered closer.

Rattray warmed to the subject: 'But this is different. It is. It's a blow at our independence. The likes of this has never been before.'

'Never.'

'And anyway he's wrong about the hands in the eightsome. Of course he is. I question if he knows . . .'

Jock grew reticent, and modest. He scratched his head and blew out his cheeks. He was in a tricky position. But no one would say that Jock let them down. He would see to that. They spoke more freely. They repeated some of the Colonel's more irrelevant questions, and it was the first time that Jock had allowed himself the luxury of listening. Every criticism of Barrow was for him another flattery. But he did not seem to lead them on: indeed, he protested that they should not make it difficult for him. Even the doctor was bewildered by his display, and it was generally supposed in the Mess that a knowledge of physiology gave the doctor an insight into human motive and character beyond his fellow officers.

'Aye,' Jock said thoughtfully. 'Off parade's off parade, right enough.'

Many of the officers had to leave before the end, but the cronies stayed and half an hour later they were winking at each other. Jock had been like a lamb since the first night the Colonel arrived. He had done just what Morag had advised him, and he had kept clear of the Mess. But now he kept tapping his fingers on a knee that was scarred with battle wounds.

SIX

Jimmy Cairns said nothing to the Colonel as they made their way over to the Naafi canteen to inspect it. The Colonel was investigating some rumours about pilfering. He was his usual cool and efficient self, and he treated his Adjutant almost as if he were a private secretary. He turned to him constantly asking him to make a note of some detail. But on their way back to H.Q. block, Jimmy lifted his eyes from the ground and looked the Colonel in the face for the first time that afternoon. He was much too honest a man to harbour something in his heart for long. He liked to get things into the open.

'Colonel?'

'Jimmy?'

'I'm afraid they won't like it, sir.'

'Who? The Naafi people? They're not meant to.'

'No, sir; you know fine who I mean.' The low afternoon sun, shimmering red through the cloud, dazzled him as he spoke.

The Colonel stopped and put his hands on his hips. He frowned, and moved his moustache.

'You mean the officers?'

'Yes, sir.'

'I wouldn't do it unless I thought it were necessary.'

'But, Colonel, it's almost an insult. Some of them have been dancing for thirty years or more.'

'I'm afraid it's an order.' The Colonel started forward again, but Jimmy persevered.

'Surely the officers above field rank might be . . .'

'I said it was an order.' The Colonel's voice was low and icy. Then he stretched his neck and went on in his usual tone. 'There; the windows in that block could do with a wash. I suppose it's all this snow. What's the building used for?'

'Band Block, sir.' Jimmy answered absently.

'I see.'

The Regimental Sergeant-Major was standing just inside the door to H.Q. and he came noisily to a salute, bringing all the corporals and orderlies in the vicinity to attention.

'Party—party 'shun!'

'Mr Riddick?'

'Sir.' The voice was thick and immensely loud.

'Please ask the Pipe-Major to come and see me.'

The R.S.M. despatched an orderly to fetch Mr McLean straight away. He then retired to his office and removing his bonnet called for his cup of tea. Nothing delighted him more than that the Pipe-Major should be on the carpet. It seemed to him that during Jock's term of office the pipes and drums had been granted too many privileges. But then Mr Riddick had no more music in him than Major Charlie Scott.

When the Adjutant and the Colonel walked into the Colonel's office they were surprised to find Jock there. The Colonel was more than surprised; he was irritated. Nobody had any right to enter his office in his absence. Jock turned and nodded: he was still flushed from his conversation in the Mess and he was spoiling for a battle, but the Colonel still managed to keep his patience. He held his stick in both hands and glanced down at it.

'Hullo, Jock,' he said with a stiff informality.

Jock rolled his eyes. 'Do I intrude?'

The Colonel said, 'Don't go, Jimmy,' and Cairns closed the door behind him. He would have much preferred to leave, and although he was not a man to look at the ceiling or at the floor, he could not make up his mind whether he would be right to meet Barrow's eye, or Jock's. He glanced from one to the other, and fidgeted. Barrow laid his stick on his desk and walked briskly round to his chair.

'What can we do for you?'

Jock turned, almost pirouetted:

'I was wondering if you wanted me this afternoon.'

'Oh, thank you very much.' The Colonel was both serious and polite. 'I don't think there are any more queries just at present. I'm afraid it must all be a terrible bore for you, just now.'

'Bore?' Jock was at his most infuriating. 'Bore? A-huh. What have you been up to, the day?'

The Colonel unlocked the drawer of his desk and brought out his leather blotter and some papers. It was the sort of blotter a boy is given by a grandparent who shops at Fortnum's. He had kept it for many years. He turned over some papers, pretending to concentrate on them, and took his reading glasses from his tunic pocket. He buttoned the pocket carefully before laying the case down just beyond the blotter, on the desk. He did not feel like telling Jock the exact purpose of his inspection.

'Jimmy and I have been running through some of that fire drill. I noticed on the map that there aren't any extinguishers in the body of the Naafi.'

Jock replied indignantly. 'There are three or four there. I mind them fine.'

'Really? They're not on the chart.'

He looked at Jimmy, who nodded in agreement and who was about to say something when Jock interrupted.

'I was never good at the paper work, Colonel. But you'll find them there right enough. Is that not right, Jimmy?'

Jimmy nodded. He was again about to speak when the Colonel cut in. 'Oh, quite right. We've just been over and checked.' He smiled. 'I don't enjoy the paper work either.'

'I would have thought that Whitehall gave a man a taste for it.'

'Curzon Street, as a matter of fact. Well, Jock, thanks for calling in. I mustn't keep you.' The Colonel would not have put it as clumsily as that had he not intended the hint to be translated as an order. But Jock paused, his weight thrown on one foot. His words did not come as he had intended them to. They came in an almost apologetic rush.

'This . . . eh . . . This dancing caper. You don't expect me to turn up, do you?'

Jimmy felt suddenly cold. He glanced at the Colonel who had removed his glasses.

'All officers.'

Jock hesitated, smiled sourly.

'It's not on, boy.'

The Colonel replaced his glasses and fingered his papers

again. But he did not use his artillery. He spoke lightly like
a nanny.

'I'm not much looking forward to 7.15 myself. But I think
we'd best all turn up.'

Jock's smile had changed to something nearer a sneer. He
spoke more rudely than he had dared before. 'Is that an order,
when you say you think we'd best all turn up?'

'If you like to put it that way.'

Jimmy moved the handle of the door, but Jock still hesitated. He walked back a step or two towards the desk and
he spoke in quite a different tone of voice. He was pleading.

'Look here, boy, if . . .'

'Colonel. I prefer to be addressed as Colonel.' His voice
was raised and now Jock, too, grew angry. 'Very well then,
Colonel. If I and some . . .'

'If I may suggest; some other time.' The Colonel did not
look up, and Jock was badly stung. He clenched his fists. His
colour rose. Then he straightened up.

'O.K., Colonel,' he said through his teeth. 'O.K.'

He made a great business of the final salute, smashing his
heels together, and Barrow nodded. As he had no hat on,
he was not called to return the salute. Jock did not look at
Cairns as he marched out. He did not look at anybody: he
did not even remember to return Mr Riddick's salute as he
passed through the lobby. He looked neither to left or right.
He marched.

Much to the R.S.M.'s disappointment, Mr McLean was
faultlessly dressed; and he did not look perturbed. Then
he never did. Mr Riddick gave a phlegmy cough, about
turned, and knocked on the Colonel's door.

'March in, Mr McLean.' He tried to make it sound as
near to an order as possible. 'March in.'

The Pipe-Major walked into the room and he came to a
halt without making much noise about it. He did not bang
his feet on the ground.

Mr Riddick was listening at the door, but his face soon
wore a disappointed expression. The Colonel was explaining
to the Pipe-Major just how he wanted the officers to dance
and he was speaking in a friendly way.

'Oh yes, sir.' Mr McLean sounded like a friendly game-keeper. 'Oh yes; we'll manage that, sir.'

'Have you a piper competent to do the job?'

'All the pipers are good, sir. They're a good band. But I think I had better go along myself. It will make it easier, I'm thinking.' There was just a wash of the Atlantic in his voice.

'You needn't if there's somebody else.'

'Well, if I can't some morning, then we'll send along Corporal Fraser. He's tactful, you know.'

'Very good, Pipe-Major.'

'Thank you, sir.' The Pipe-Major seemed to want to go on talking. 'It is a while since we have had a subalterns' parade of this sort, though Colonel Sinclair once suggested it would be a good idea.'

'It isn't only the subalterns, you understand.'

'Oh? But surely the senior officers . . .'

The Colonel looked annoyed. He touched his moustache. 'The order affects all officers.'

'All the officers. I see, sir.' The Pipe-Major sighed. It was time he left. But as he turned the Colonel said:

'I'm not a great one for spit and polish, Pipe-Major, but the windows of your Band Block could do with a wash.' He said this quite pleasantly, and Mr McLean looked concerned.

'Oh, aye, sir. We'll get that seen to straight away, sir; straight away.' Then he smiled uncertainly, and the Colonel smiled back.

'Straight away.'

'Right this minute, sir. Thank you very much, sir.'

'That will be all.'

The Pipe-Major nearly knocked over Mr Riddick when he opened the door. The eavesdropper moved his feet sharply, and coughed. 'Cup-a-tea for you, Mr McLean?'

'Thank you, Mr Riddick. That would be fine,' the Pipe-Major replied in his comfortable way and they went into the little office. But as they closed the door behind them, order-lies in the next room raised their eyebrows and shrugged. It was never a good idea for these two to get together. Even in the Mess the sergeants did not trust them in the same game of *Housey-housey*. It always ended in the same way.

When they took off their bonnets it could be seen that both men were a little bald, but while Mr Riddick's hair was quite grey Mr McLean's was sandy in colour. They sat silently for a while; then the R.S.M. launched straight into the meat of the matter.

'Captain Cairns was in here this afternoon talkin' about this dancing class. Said he had half a mind to chuck up the adjutancy.'

'Aye?' Mr McLean took five lumps.

'Told him not to be daft. I've seen a change of colonel before today and there's always trouble.'

'A change is usually for the better. That's true in life.' Mr McLean enjoyed universals, but they were not for the R.S.M.

'Don't know anything about that. But I do know it would be damned disloyal to march off now. As Adjutant he has responsibilities, same as the rest of us.'

'Aye. But it's a big change for him. He's known Jock all the way from El Alamein.'

'That's not the point. I can tell you, Mr McLean—I wouldn't express an opinion to anyone else, mind you— but I can tell you, this one'll be the better Colonel. Better by far. Shall I tell you why, eh?'

It was the beginning. The expression on the Pipe-Major's face did not change, but he said gently, 'I don't think I'll be agreeing with you here.' He nodded his head. Mr McLean was anxious that it should be a pleasant chat.

'Right,' the R.S.M. said. 'I'll tell you why he's the better Colonel. Because he's a gentleman.'

Mr McLean smiled a wise smile and the R.S.M. repeated himself more emphatically, with just a flicker of malice in his boss eye.

'Because he's a gentleman.'

Slowly came the reply. 'You're the terrible snob, Mr Riddick. It is always the same with you people who start in the Brigade of Guards. You're such terrible snobs; it is wicked.' As he grew angry, he spoke more quickly.

'Mr McLean. I know what I'm saying.' The R.S.M. poured out another cup of tea and passed his hand over his short thin hair. He made a sour face. 'Rankers may make Quarter-masters. But believe you me, sir, they don't make battalion commanders.' "Sir," from one Warrant Officer to another is a gauntlet.

'That's lies. Jock was the most successful Battalion Commander in the war.'

'The war was a different sort of thing. You're arguing off the point, again, Mr McLean. Of course he's a good soldier, no one denies it; but the point is that he should be in my job or yours. And I'm not the sort of man who ought to command the Battalion.'

Mr McLean controlled himself.

'Ah well,' he said, 'we shall see what we shall see.' Then he added, in spite of himself, 'But I think it is Jock who should have been appointed.'

Mr Riddick was in a keen mood. He wagged his nobbly finger.

'The very fact that we call him Jock . . . Och, you must see it.'

Suddenly Mr McLean was unleashed. He spoke quickly. 'You're a diehard Tory; yes, and it's you that stirs up class hatreds.'

Mr Riddick pushed back his shoulders. 'That's a damned impudent thing to say, Mr McLean.'

'It is true. Yes it is.'

'I never knew we had a bloody Communist as Pipe-Major.'

The R.S.M. now stood up and towered above the round figure of Mr McLean, who half closed his eyes, and half whispered, half shouted his reply. 'I have told you before, I am a Liberal, Mr Riddick. A Whig, a Whig, a Whig!'

Rather patchily the R.S.M.'s complexion was changing from blue to vermilion.

'It's an unwritten rule in this Battalion, Mr McLean, that politics will not be discussed. I'd bring that to your attention.'

'Och, you and your rules. It's playing at soldiers that you are.'

'Pipe-Major; I'm reminding you of my rank.' Mr Riddick put on his bonnet. He was shouting now.

'And a man of your rank should know better than to

accuse one of his colleagues of being a Communist, when he's a Whig. You had best go back to your Grenadiers or whatever it was.'

'Are you attemptin' to insult my late regiment? Tell me that, Mr McLean.' Mr Riddick's voice was low and menacing, but the Pipe-Major after several years of practice, knew just how far he could go. He put on his bonnet and prepared to leave.

'No,' he said.

'If you want to insult my late regiment then I think we'd better meet in the gymnasium.'

The Pipe-Major smiled and shook his head.

'Peter Pan; that's what we should call you, Mr Riddick. Man, we're far too old to be meeting in the gymnasium. You'd better go home now. Muffin the Mule's on in a few moments.'

'By God, you're a bloody impudent man. I've a mind to put you under close arrest. D'you hear me? March you right inside.'

'Then it's high time I was leaving. Mr Riddick, I am thanking you for my cup of tea. It has been invigorating.'

But the R.S.M. did not return his smile.

'Pipe-Major, I observed when marching by today that the windows of the Band Block are in a dirty condition.'

'Did you, now?' The Pipe-Major's eyebrows nearly touched the fringe of his hair. 'Well, I'll tell you what, Mr Riddick, I'll go right back there now and see that they are cleaned, just for your sake. That's what I'll be doing.'

Shortly after the Pipe-Major left, the R.S.M. spotted a soldier with the lace of his boot undone. He was put on a charge for being improperly dressed, straight away. He was lucky not to be put in gaol.

SEVEN

Now the town was small, but the county was smaller. The news of the dancing class soon circulated and seasoned officers blushed like cadets when they were asked if they had learnt their *Pas-de-Basques* yet. Underneath the layer of sunburn even Sandy Macmillan grew a little warm, but if the officers were teased, the county notwithstanding was thoroughly glad. It was a sign for the better. The officers from Campbell Barracks had not made themselves popular over the preceding year or two, with their drinking and their springy dancing. Even those people in the county who did not consider themselves to be purists were a little sick of them. At the Hunt Ball, not that there is much of a Hunt, people had grown accustomed, in an angry sort of way, to seeing the officers form up in front of the band so that the rest of the dancers were edged down to the bottom of the set. They clapped their hands and joked with the drummer, and they hooched and swung their women.

Everybody knew that Jock Sinclair encouraged them: as acting Colonel he was at the root of the trouble, for this is an old axiom: that a Mess takes on the complexion of its Colonel. It was therefore with warm hearts that the county welcomed a man who was instantly recognizable as a gentleman—Barrow Boy.

At first people were curious to meet him; then they were anxious; then, after a month, they were desperate. The county began to talk of nothing else and everybody wished they could peep over the sixteen-foot wall. Rumours abounded. All sorts of innocent tweed-coated men were recognized as the mysterious Colonel. Jimmy Cairns's aunt in Crieff set the Victorian terraces alight with her news items straight from the Adjutant's mother's mouth. A young farmer who had something to do with one of the Territorial outfits in the neighbourhood swore that Barrow was the White Rabbit himself. Barrow had blown up the heavy water plant in wherever-it-was; he had been one of Winston's special boys. Barrow had made the officers run round the barracks before breakfast. Barrow had been doing far rougher things to the idle than any young Alexander. Barrow had been in Colditz. Barrow had said that if any officer held his knife like a pen he would be posted to another regiment. Barrow was the talk of both town and county.

'He's a small man. You never see him in uniform this side of the wall. My dear, he has a look of Lawrence of Arabia.'

'Lawrence of where?'

'Nonsense . . . his eyes are much larger.'

'He's coming to dinner on Thursday,' proudly: that was said with pride.

'Really?' and that said with chagrin.

'Well probably. You must recall him. Tom knew him before the war. You must remember him.'

'My dear, I was a child then.'

In the county the talk is well up to standard. And the county often meets, even when the roads are bad. There were cocktail parties in houses which once had known stronger drinks and fuller servants' quarters, but here as ever gossip, like a leaf, whirled round and round, then with a spiral movement and on the hot breath of a matron, it was lifted upwards to unlikely heights.

'Oh, for Christ's sake,' Jock said, when he heard or overheard such a conversation, and he clenched his fists and screwed up his face. But he never got further than that: instead he cracked that joke of his about red tabs and tits, which usually went down very well. He did not like to hear much talk of the Colonel; he said all the talk at the parties was childish; people going on as if the boy were Monty himself. 'Oh, for Christ's sake,' he said.

'He's English, you know.'

'Nonsense. He's a connection of the jute Maclarens.'

'Dundee?'

'Originally.'

'Really? He has money?'

'I don't know how much now.'

The ladies talked about him most at the cocktail parties, but in the swells' club in the town and after dinner in some of the houses that still ran to dinner parties (proper style) his name came up again. The men treated it with a little more reserve.

'Was he with the First Battalion?'

'Can't have been. Billy would have met him.'

'He was S.A.S., wasn't he?'

Then the older voice. 'Only thing I know about him is he's got a pair of Purdeys, and they say he can shoot with them: that's more than that tyke Sinclair can do, at all events.'

A 'hear, hear,' a finishing of the glass, a moment or two spent in clearing away the dishes for the foreign girl, and it is time to join the ladies.

But the Colonel did not go to the dinner on the Thursday or on the Friday or to supper on the Sunday. He had to stack his invitations horizontally on his shelf, but he still replied to them all in his own neat hand. Each time he refused, and he gave as his reason pressure of work.

When at last, a month later, he invited the whole neighbourhood to a regimental cocktail party it was no surprise to anyone that there was hardly a refusal. The county had decided to come to the Colonel. And the drink had better be good.

And the drink was good. Whatever may be said about that Battalion's fighting record or social performance no one but a Plymouth Sister could deny the quality of the drinks at one of the regimental parties. There were all sorts of drinks, and there were a great many of them. The officers saw that the stewards circulated amongst the guests swiftly and for a long time. It was impossible to hold an empty glass, and, perhaps consequently, it was impossible to believe that the party was not a howling success. Simpson and some of the other better-known young men were like perfect ushers at a wedding. They welcomed people as soon as they arrived in the ante-room, and they offered plates of savouries and silver boxes of cigarettes to two hundred guests. At the beginning—he'd had one for the road—Jock was pink in the eyes with social affability and he was holding guests

male or female by the elbow, pretending to be listening to
what they had to say. But often he glanced through the door
to the hall where Barrow was greeting the guests.

Barrow made a point of shaking everybody's hand. He
had the dazed and silvery look of the bride's father, and
as he shook hands he said a word or two; then, as the
guest replied, his eyes wandered to the next guest in the
long queue. Everybody looked at him as if he were a waxwork
that could talk, and although some of the sharper females
dared a personal question, nobody was any the wiser at the
completion of the ceremony.

The ante-room itself was very pleasant. Some of the worst
armchairs and wicker tables had been moved out for the
occasion. The tartan and the tweeds toned with the panelling
of the walls and the wood toned well with the whisky. The
chandeliers and the tumblers sparkled and the Mess servants
made friends with some of the grand ladies which, after all,
is always a sign of a good party.

The same grand ladies, when they were not making friends
with the Mess servants or keeping Sandy Macmillan at a safe
distance, concentrated on the Colonel. Some waited in their
corners until he came to them while others, a little older and
a little keener, moved through the throng to meet him. They
all had a shot at penetrating his defences. Only one person had
anything like a success, and she wished she had not spoken.

'You ought to have had a girl friend to keep you company
when you greeted us in the hall.'

A slight smile: 'Yes? My Adjutant offered to help.'

'We've got lots of presentable girls you know: you'd be
surprised.'

'Really?'

'We'll get you a wife.'

'As a matter of fact I have had one of those.'

'Oh. Oh, really?' The girl put her weight back on one
heel.

But it only added to the mystery of the man.

Even Morag had a try at opening the oyster. She was in
her smartest cherry hat—one with a snout to it—and
she wore a black tailored coat and court shoes. The Colonel
found her alone, and he recognized her again, immediately.

She refused a cigarette from his little silver case; it was one
of those old-fashioned cases with a curve in it to fit closely
to chest or hip. Morag was standing alone, not because she
did not know anybody there, but because she liked to stand
alone when she was not enjoying herself. Several officers had
come to make conversation to her, but she frightened them
away. Simpson tried valiantly.

'What a smart hat!'

'This thing?'

'It's awfully smart.'

'Och, I picked it up in the sales for one-and-nine.' Morag
did not smile. Her common sense was almost militant.

'How clever of you,' Simpson replied pleasantly, but the
answer was as sharp as before.

'Not very. It's just common sense. If you get up early
enough you get the bargains.'

'I think I'd be frightened to death. All those women
fighting for the best bargain.'

'Oh yes.' She looked at him as if she thought him stupid,
and he offered her some snacks, but she had no time for
them.

'Too fattening?' Simpson suggested with a smile, and she
replied, 'I wouldn't know about that.'

After that he was stuck with her for a little time and they
talked about some of the other people near them. Then she
said, 'You'd better go and give them their sardines,' and not
with grace, but with relief, he took his opportunity.

But she was more forthcoming with the Colonel, who did
not make the mistake of flattering her.

'D'you enjoy things like this?' she asked him, and before
he had time to reply she said, 'Neither do I,' and he smiled.

'They serve a purpose, I suppose.'

'Colonel Barrow, I don't fancy it's the time or place . . .'
she said, and she hesitated. Barrow's mouth tightened a little, and he looked at her severely. But nothing could stop
Morag when she wanted to say something. She was as firm
as the regimental Douglas Jackson.

'Whatever Father's said, don't think I don't see how difficult it must be for you. . . .' But there was no getting closer
to the Colonel. He leant back on his heel, and looked round

the room. She only saw the side of his face when he replied, 'How kind of you to say so. You mustn't worry.'

'I wanted to say that.'

'I'm grateful to you. Now, have you met . . .' But as the Colonel looked round for a spare subaltern, Jock shouldered his way closer. He flicked his head at Barrow.

'Aye. You've met Morag?'

The Colonel looked nervous. 'Oh yes. Delighted.' He waved his glass and nodded. 'If you'll excuse me.' He picked his way through the crowd rather as if he were frightened of it. Two or three groups opened like a flower to let the queen bee land, but he hovered and moved on again, farther round the room. His face was the face of anxiety. But that again only endeared him to the ladies.

Sometimes, and all of a sudden, they felt that it was only right that he should be called Boy. In spite of the grey hair, he looked like a child at a party; looked as if he had lost his way. And that, to regimental women, is something very attractive: their own husbands are always so vehement in protesting that they know where they are going. When Jock saw one of these take him by the hand and draw him into a group, it sickened him.

'Well, Father?' He had said nothing to Morag.

'A-huh. Well, you seemed to be talking with him very seriously.'

'I was just warning him what a bear you are.'

'Aye. What did you say?'

'Nothing.'

'Well you looked bloody pleased about it. He's no the Brigadier you know; he's just another colonel.'

Morag looked angry. The muscle in her cheek moved and she looked down at her feet.

'I meant no harm,' she said. 'For goodness sake.'

'Look at them now: look at them. You know these are the same women that made such a bloody fuss over me in forty-five. But I couldn't cope with them. You wouldn't remember. I was bloody rude to them.'

'I'm sure,' she replied, tightly.

Because some of the best-behaved subalterns and their blonde partners asked him politely, if persistently like little children, the Colonel allowed them to dance in the main hall, and the pipers were duly organized. Most of the grown-ups left about then which, as things turned out, was a blessing for Barrow; but the rest of them really settled down to enjoy themselves. In the billiards room, one or two of the wives were all blouse and colour by now, and Dusty Millar was very drunk, but Jock and some of the others came through in a group, abreast, towards the dancing. Morag stayed until the pipers arrived. They both knew her and smiled politely, but in spite of Douglas Jackson's grip on her arm, she stayed no longer.

The Colonel disappeared into the ante-room once again, when the dancing began. But later, as the noise in the hall increased, he grew more and more nervy and two or three times he ignored altogether remarks put to him by his guests. The noise from the hall grew in gusts and it was soon clear that the style of dancing was diverging very far from the lines laid down by the Pipe-Major at the early morning classes. Seeing the Colonel's face, nobody in the ante-room could think of anything else and the whole Mess seemed to be shaking.

Suddenly Barrow could stand it no longer. It was as if he had known all along that the party was building up to this. He detached himself from the group by the fire and walked out of the room: then he checked himself. When he saw the scene in the hall he grew pale with anger, and the liquor circled even faster in his glass. There were two sets dancing the eightsome. The first was lively, but their behaviour was excusable at the end of such a party. That could not be said for the second. Jock, Douglas Jackson, Rattray, and a fourth who was a local farmer, were the men in the set, and they were hoping that the Colonel would come to watch. Three or four times Jimmy Cairns, dancing in the other set, had implored them to dance less noisily. But he had done so in vain.

Barrow's lip twitched and he rubbed his thumb against the tips of his fingers. The whole floor was shaking, and the glass in the front door was rattling as the dancers leapt about the room swinging, swaying and shouting. When they saw the Colonel the noise increased, and a moment later Rattray

inadvertently let go of the partner he was swinging vigorously so that she spun like a top across the floor, lost her balance,
and fell. She fell at Barrow's feet.

Corporal Fraser and the other piper stopped playing and
the dance came suddenly to an end. The Colonel reached
forward to help the girl and she shook her hair from her
face. She was too uncertain of the look in Barrow's eyes to
say anything at all and Jock was the first to speak.

'Are you all right, lassie?'

But it was Barrow who spoke next. His voice was low and
clear.

'Mr Rattray. I believe you owe this young lady an apology.'

'Oh hell . . .' she began. She was a student from St.
Andrews, this girl, and she knew all the words, but when
she looked at the Colonel again her vocabulary failed her,
and her voice died away. The Colonel stood very tensely. The
gin in his glass was shaking so violently now that it splashed,
and when Jock observed that a little of it had spilt he looked
at the Colonel's face, and he smiled a half-triumphant smile.

'Have a drink, boy, have a drink,' he said cordially; then
he half turned towards the others. 'Unless you'd like to join
us. I'm sure Douglas here'll stand out.'

Barrow's voice was a pitch or two higher than usual.

'Piper: this will be the last reel.'

'Sir.'

The Colonel stood and watched as the pipers played again.
He took a gulp of his drink to empty the shaking glass. The
dance began quietly, to Jimmy Cairns's great relief, and the
girls soon adapted themselves to the style of it. They held
their heads high and their backs arched: they placed their
hands firmly with the palms downwards before them when
it came to a swing. Barrow's shoulders dropped an inch with
relief.

But when it was Jock's turn in the centre he let his bloodshot eyes rest on the Colonel by the door. For the first circle
he behaved himself: he set to his partner and to the third
lady, and he completed the figure of eight with reserved precision coming near to perfection. Then when they circled
again he sprang off the ground, flung his hands high in the

air and let out a scream to crack rock. The others followed
his lead. The noise rose, the floor started to shake again,
and the glass in the door rattled louder than before.

The Colonel's voice rose above it all; and he was collected
no longer.

'Sinclair! Sinclair! Stop the dancing. D'you hear me,
Piper? Stop at once!'

He looked sick. Hearing the commotion people emerged
from the cloakrooms and the ante-room to witness a scene
such as the Mess had not known in forty years. But Jock
had never looked so foursquare. He stood in the middle of
the dancers and there was still the suspicion of a smile lurk-
ing behind the bland expression of his face. Embarrassed by
the silence, one or two people in a mumbling sort of way
endeavoured to interrupt, but the Colonel snapped at them
to keep silent. One of the girls who had spoken blushed with
indignation.

Jock's voice was low when he spoke.

'You called me, Colonel?'

'I did. I'll see you tomorrow. Tomorrow. I'll . . . Pipers,
we've had enough of this. Quite enough.' Barrow fidgeted
as he spoke, and although Jock was just a few yards in front
of him, he was shouting. Then there was quiet. The dancers
moved, and the pipers marched smartly out of the frozen
world. Corporal Fraser looked upset, almost guilty, as if he
had seen those things which a good piper should not see.

Now, for the first time the Colonel looked around him and
he looked afraid and bewildered as if he had awoken from a
dream and found himself at his own trial. He sighed heavily,
and stretched his fingers.

Jock stared at him quite steadily, with victorious calm.
He did not quite have the audacity to say, 'Are you going
to rap me over the knuckles, Colonel?' but he thought of
doing so. Instead, he grinned openly at the dancers around
him.

Barrow now turned to the guests. 'The party's over. It's
late. It's very late. I'm sorry it should end like this.'

Jimmy came to the rescue. 'It's time we all had something
to eat . . .' he said with a friendly smile, but Douglas Jackson
was not smiling. He had not moved, and he stood on the

floor with one foot planted before the other, and his hands on his hips, in a Highlander's pose.

'We were just beginning to enjoy ourselves, Colonel.' It might have been a reasonable enough thing to have said, but Jackson had once before spoken out too boldly.

The Colonel checked himself, and everybody waited again. Jock was now grinning openly. Slowly the Colonel turned his head.

'Who said that?' And he knew perfectly well.

'I did.'

'Adjutant!'

Jimmy was trying to steady everybody. He nodded and moved up to the Colonel.

'Not now,' he whispered, but the Colonel braced his head back.

'Do as you're told. Take his name. Take that officer's name.'

'Yes, sir.' Jimmy said. Of course he knew the name, so he did not move and two or three people in the room began to giggle. Jackson, for all his impudence, was looking very white himself now and he stared at the Colonel unblinkingly. The onlookers were fascinated by the scene, and apart from the two women who giggled, they were petrified by it. In the hall, they stood quite still. But in the doorway through to the ante-room people were shoving and craning their necks to see better. Just in the same way that speeches are passed back in a crowd too large, a commentary of the scene was passed as far as the billiards room and the dining-room where some of the servants stood, their heads on one side, to hear more clearly.

But it was all over. The Colonel turned quickly away and walked towards the cloakroom, while some of the others went up to talk to Jock and Jackson. Jock laughed and shook his head, but Jackson was still very white. As some of his cronies congratulated him he stuck out his chin a little further.

'I was in my rights,' he said, then he swore a little, but he did not relax enough to smile. In a moment when they were still standing about the hall the Colonel reappeared again, with his coat and bonnet on. He stopped by the front door, and putting on his gloves, he lifted his head and said:

'Good-night, all.'

One or two replied 'good-night', but the door had not closed behind him when the laughter began to ring round the room. Jimmy was sweating now: he was suddenly angry, and he tried to shout them down, but Jock was leading the laughter, and they paid no attention to him. They laughed all the louder when Jimmy grabbed his bonnet and ran out after the Colonel.

EIGHT

He jumped into the jeep beside the Colonel just before he drove off, and the Colonel said nothing to him. Instead, he let in the clutch and accelerated fast. He changed his gears swiftly, like an expert, and he took the corners round the square as if he were racing. He braked hard at the gate and Jimmy shouted 'Colonel' to the sentry, who stood aside. By the time he had presented arms, the jeep was clear of the barracks.

In the Mess, the remainder—to use Mr Riddick's term for any party which had lost some of its members, the remainder moved to the billiards room where the drink was handy on the table, and as they drank, each one of them grew more like himself. Jock began to sweat. Douglas Jackson grew harsher until he had no time for any man or any idea except stern discipline. Rattray grew more vehement about Barrow's English accent, and the need for a Gaelic revival. Dusty Millar told story after story. The doctor was sitting on the step by the leather bench, like a mouse with a lot of hair. He said, 'It's surely significant that the quarrel should have revolved round such a primitive thing as folk dancing.'

This united them.

'Och, chuck it, Doc,' Jock said irritably.

'You and your Freud and all that Sassenach cock,' Rattray said, and Dusty Millar echoed Jock.

'Aye, chuck it, Doc. For chuck's sake chuck it.'

'What'll I say the morn, eh?' Jock said. 'What'll I tell him?' and they began to make suggestions.

The Colonel drove for several miles and the cold night air rushing into the jeep did not leave Jimmy breath for any words of comfort. They drove fast out on the south road, which is wide and straight. But in the dips there were patches of fog, and two or three times Jimmy was sure they were bound for the ditch. A wisp appeared in the yellow light of the headlamp, another, then they were driving through a yellow wall. In a second they were clear again and Jimmy sighed and folded his arms to try and protect himself from the bitter cold. At last, quite suddenly, Barrow took his foot off the accelerator and the jeep slowed down; then, out of gear, it glided to rest at the side of the road. Barrow eased himself back in the seat.

'What a childish thing to do,' he said and he closed his eyes.

His eyelashes were long and they came to rest on his cheek with a peculiar softness.

Jimmy said, 'Och, I don't blame you. It's one way of getting something out of your system. Though if I'd known the speed you were going to travel I'm not so sure I'd have come for the joy-ride.'

The Colonel smiled faintly. 'Childish.'

'That fog's nasty. But you can certainly drive a jeep.' The compliment did not encourage the Colonel. He sat still, with his eyes shut, and Jimmy went on. 'And it's bloody cold too. You've got a coat on but I'm frozen stiff. With this kilt blowing about I'm not sure I'm all here, any more.' He went on talking for a moment or two, saying nothing, but speaking in a voice of persuasive comfort and complete normality. At last the Colonel opened his eyes, and he began to move out of the jeep.

'You drive,' he said. 'I'm in no state to drive.'

'Have you had a couple?' Jimmy said, moving into the driver's seat as Barrow walked round to the other door.

'It takes more than a couple to make a man of my age make a fool of himself.'

'Och, people always do bloody silly things at Mess parties. It's part of the tradition. I know somebody who once had . . .'

'Not a Colonel.'

'A colonel's human, isn't he? He has a heart?'

'He shouldn't have: only a complexion.' Then he seemed to withdraw into his own world.

'Drive on,' he said at last. 'Drive on.' And taking it quite gently, Jimmy drove back to the cobbled streets. The street lamps had haloes round them like moons and there was no traffic on the road. But Jimmy never went in for dramatic gear-changing or fast cornering. He obeyed the law, and in the town they drove at under thirty miles an hour. He glanced at the Colonel who was staring straight in front of him. His expression was the expression of a boy being driven back to a boarding school he hates.

'I think we'd best drop into the Station and get a bite to eat.'

Barrow nodded, and bit his moustache. Jimmy had run out of conversation now. He drew up in the big yard outside the hotel and switched off the engine. Then he saw that Barrow had pitched forward and he was holding his head in his hand.

'Ridicule's always the finish. You know that?'

'Who said anything about ridicule?'

Barrow wagged his head irritably, and Jimmy found more words.

'For God's sake, Colonel. They behaved bloody badly and you'd the sense to get out. What's wrong in that?'

Barrow seemed to like that idea. He clung to it, again childlike.

'Is that how it looked?'

'That's how it was.'

They climbed out and Barrow breathed in deeply as they walked to the hotel door. 'I say, thanks awfully,' he said.

'For what?'

'For coming along like this. You know . . .'

'It's part of the service, Colonel; part of the service.'

As the Colonel ate his meal Jimmy was keen to find excuses for him. They sat in the far corner of the large dining-room, on opposite sides of a small table. Jimmy rested his arms on the table leaning forward to listen to Barrow, and to talk to him in a low voice.

'What was your job down in Whitehall? I never found that out.'

The Colonel smiled his former weary but collected smile.

'I gathered Jock had found out everything about me.'

'Oh no. Eton and Oxford was as far as he got.'

'That's not strictly true, either.'

'So?' Jimmy leant farther forward.

'I was only at school for a term or two. I had a private tutor most of the time.'

Jimmy nodded. He said with sympathy, 'Aye. Were you sick?'

'No.' The Colonel ate another mouthful before replying. 'My people thought it was a better idea.' The Colonel busied himself with the wine list. He felt uncomfortable. 'Sounds strange, I know.'

'Not all that.' Jimmy shook his head. 'Hell, I might as well not have gone to school at all. I spent half my time playing games in class and all that. I never listened to the teacher.' There was a likeness between Jimmy and Jock which people often noticed. They were both heavy men, although Jimmy was only in his middle thirties, and they had the same forthright manner. But Jimmy smiled much more. As Adjutant he behaved to the subalterns much as a friendly sales manager behaves towards his representatives. He joked them into doing things. But he was not capable of the same sort of banter this evening. When he remembered his academy days he smiled, but he soon grew serious again. It was like him, just as it would have been unlike Jock, to fall in with the Colonel's suggestion that they drink a bottle of claret. He certainly would not have noticed had he been served with a glass of burgundy instead, but it was quite obvious that Barrow was something of an expert, and Jimmy drew him on the subject. Then at last he returned to the subject of the Colonel's previous employment. Barrow shrugged.

'Most of my time was spent with M.I.5.'

'That must have been a terrible strain.'

The Colonel nodded. He did not seem to want to discuss his work. 'It was quite enjoyable: I suppose it took a lot out of one.' But it had not been as adventurous as it sounded.

'I'm sure it did. Whatever they say it's that nervous work, and brain work too, that tires a man out. Did you have much leave before you came up here?'

'Ten days.'

Jimmy smiled. 'And you wonder why you were a bit ratty tonight? Ten days is not enough. It seems to me you've been very patient.'

'There were actually other things . . .' The Colonel looked up doubtfully, and Jimmy was staring at him with solemn sympathy. 'I had a marriage you know. I had a wife.'

'I'm sorry.'

'Oh, it's all over now really. But that was one of the reasons I accepted this job, you know: a change. I'd been rather lonely, I suppose.' He paused, and started again. 'I think perhaps all of us who were prisoners in the East are a little cranky now. D'you think that?'

'Och no,' Jimmy said, into his glass.

'No? I do. All of us who were in Jap hands. That's what my wife believed, anyway. She was quite sure of it. She had a friend too, whose husband . . . well, there are hundreds of examples. I suppose we got a touch of the sun. Or . . .' Quite suddenly he decided not to go on. He just stopped.

Jimmy moved his glass in a little circle, on the tablecloth, and some cigarette ash piled up beside it.

'Och,' he said, 'a change of colonel always takes time. When the next man comes along it'll be just the same.' And the Colonel leant back. He finished his claret and collected himself.

'Oh, good heavens, yes,' he said. 'You mustn't pay too much attention to me. These damned social things always unnerve me. But I knew before I came here what it would be like. They told me about Jock.'

'Jock's the hell of a man.'

'A great soldier.'

Jimmy said, 'You're not a dog in the manger, Colonel,' and Barrow shrugged.

'Strange,' he said. 'One man's goal can mean . . . well, quite honestly, not very much to another. I mean, I'm only here really for battalion experience. I expect in a year or two I'll . . .'

'Brigade level?'

'Well, if not, some special thing. A battalion would bore me, you know, after a while.' He seemed suddenly more confident and Jimmy was astonished at the change. It was only when they were leaving the dining-room that the buoyancy failed.

'Of course, all that's between you and me, Jimmy. You understand nothing's certain. I mean, it may turn out I never go farther at all, I . . .'

'I understand.'

'How late it is. Not a bad dinner, really.'

'Damned good, thank you.'

'No thanks, please.'

There was a smile on the face of both tigers. But then there was nearly always a smile on Mary Titterington's face. Anyhow, it was for her a little triumph that Jock should decide to call again after all that time. She bowed her head low, she swept back the door, and she followed him into the living-room. Then she went to the cupboard and brought out the bottle of whisky. It was cold after lunch; the sun had gone in and the clouds were gathering for snow again. Mary had only just been out to get some shillings for the meter, and the room was not yet warm. Jock looked at her closely, and reckoned she was looking well. It was Jock who first said that rude thing about her which best described the expression on her face: that curious smile. He said that she always looked as though she'd just had it. And Charlie said he was probably right.

Mary must have been over thirty. She came from Belfast, and she had failed to make a success of the London stage. In spite of the chiselled face, and the rather alluring expression, she had only been in one film. She had a figure that could be photographed from every angle, and had been from most, but—after all that—she came north to a repertory company. On the occasions when she had had a good night's sleep she was still capable of a first-class performance. But her soul was not so much in her face, any more: there was only this smile. And with the soul from her face, the Irish had gone from her voice. Once in a bottle, maybe, and usually near the end of it, both would suddenly return. But it was a good thing they reappeared so seldom, because Jock had little time for them: time neither for the soul, nor the Irish.

She lived in flat number 3 in a big house overlooking the park, and Jock had taken the stairs a little too quickly. He was very red, and out of breath.

'Hullo,' he said, with a roving eye, and she looked at him closely.

'Have you been drinking for long?'

'No, lass. I've not been drinking for long.'

After a struggle Jock was free of his greatcoat and he threw it over a chair in the corner. The room had been severely modernized. The tiled fireplace had been boarded in; there was wallpaper on the ceiling and on two of the walls. It was all very surprising, for the North.

'You've just been drinking all today.'

'I have not.'

'You've had a few.'

'How can you tell?'

'Your eyes.'

'That's very romantic,' Jock said, sitting down on the sofa. 'And what the hell's wrong with my eyes?'

'They're pink.'

'You're bloody rude.'

When she had poured out their drinks she put the cork back in the bottle and tucked her feet up on the sofa. She was small enough to fold into a neat parcel and she had very good legs. Jock was sitting as if he had had a very large lunch, and his stomach was full.

He said, 'You're rude. That's what you are.'

She brushed some ash from her pleated skirt and the bracelets on her arms clinked together as she tipped back her glass. Jock continued.

'Are you surprised to see me?'

She did not look in the least surprised, but she said, 'Mm.'

Jock said, 'You're looking very well.'

'I just got up.'

'You're bloody idle.'

She did not think so. 'I did two shows yesterday.'

Jock stared at her. 'What show's this?'

'*My Sister Eileen*.'

'You've done that before, haven't you?'

'Mm. It's a repertory company.'

'So they say. And you're Eileen?'

'No. I'm the other one. Ruth.'

Jock took a gulp of whisky. He watched her face closely

all the time he talked, and he was rather enjoying himself. He was surprising himself, and it seemed a very long time since he had seen her.

'Are you not sore you're not Eileen?'

'I'm too old for Eileen.'

'How old is Eileen?'

'She's twenty: or something like that.'

Jock gave a grin: then he chuckled and she looked quite angry.

'I said I was too old for Eileen.'

'But you said you weren't sore.'

'I'm not, for heaven's sake. Jock Sinclair, you haven't changed much . . . Ruth's a better part. If you'd seen the play you'd understand. You ought to come and see it.'

'Aye, maybe.' Jock poured himself out another drink, and he sniffed, because he had forgotten his handkerchief. 'Tell me, Mary. In Belfast, on a Sunday afternoon, do ladies often sit drinking whisky?'

'What the hell are you up to?'

'I asked you a civil question. Do they, now?'

'Sometimes, if it's cold and wet, I suppose.'

'It's always wet in Belfast, lassie.'

'This is just as bad. This is the end of the world.'

'It's not that. It's a very fine city.'

'Och, but the people . . .'

Jock watched her lips when she replied. Now he jerked his head to one side.

'Mary; I'll go next door and sleep if you come too. It'll save you whisky. Eh?'

She stabbed her cigarette out firmly.

'I don't do it that way. I'm not something in a fair.'

'You're just contrary. You know fine you'd . . .'

'Take a whisky with you instead.'

'Just for old times' sake.'

'To hell with old times' sake. I don't mind you calling, Jock Sinclair. But you're going to behave yourself, or it's home you go. For heaven's sake, Jock.' She looked at him kindly.

'Aye,' Jock said, leaning back again, with a sigh. 'Maybe.'

He pushed his tumbler forward again and she poured more

whisky into it, and lit another cigarette. When she inhaled the first breath of a cigarette she would tip her head back and exhale it out of nose and mouth together. Jock liked the way she smoked.

'I hear you've got a new colonel up the road,' she said.

'Yes, yes.'

She smiled again. 'Are you sore about it?' and he looked at her, then he smiled too. 'I'll put you over my knee, and not just to spank you.'

Mary was always telling Jock he was coarse. She clicked her teeth and put her shoe back on her foot. Jock looked at the foot and the stocking, then he turned his eyes to hers again.

'Who's been giving you your news?'

She stood up and walked across the room to fetch an ash-tray.

'Och, it's common knowledge. They say you had your knuckles rapped last night.'

Jock's colour rose at that. 'Aye, well they're bloody wrong. That's what they are.'

'Whatever you say.'

'I don't know who the hell's been telling you this but you've got the wrong end of the stick. It was me that said that, about rapping over the knuckles, or near enough. Who's been speaking to you, eh?'

'A friend.'

'Aye, well he's a liar too. The wee man got badly fussed and I said it; I said it kind of ironic-like—och, you wouldn't understand it.'

'Why shouldn't I understand?'

'Because you're bloody ignorant.'

'Listen to you.'

'Well what does ironic mean then, eh? D'you know?'

She did not reply to him, and after a moment he went on in a quieter voice.

'He lost his head altogether. That's what he did. He gets in an awful rage, you know; Barrow does. Aye, and he's to see me in the morning.' Jock paused again, but it was obvious that he wanted to say more on the subject. Mary could tell that from the way he washed the whisky round and round his tumbler, and watched it as it whirled. Mary had listened to a good many men's stories before this: and for a while Jock had been in the habit of telling her everything, when he went round for his evening chat.

He ran his tongue over his lips, which were cracked by the weather and all the cigarettes he had been smoking lately.

'He was cool enough this morning. I went to see him this morning. He's usually very cool you see. He's springy enough, aye, but he keeps well away from you. Nobody gets very near the Barrow Boy. That's one of the rules.'

Mary nodded sympathetically and she pulled her feet up on the sofa again so her shoe just hung on her toe. She smoked cigarettes all the time.

'On parade's on parade. But the way I dance is nothing to do with him.'

'I've never seen him.'

'Och, he's—he's a spry wee man. In the usual run I mean, but he's got a temper. He's always been famous for that. His wife couldn't cope with it, no. And it's worse 'an it used to be. But I tell you this; it'll no be of any use to him by the time I've finished tomorrow. . . . I've got friends in the War Office, just the same as him; aye, but that's not the point.'

Jock was speaking very fast now, and he spoke right into Mary's face. He nodded and tossed his head to emphasize his independence. 'I'll tell you. I've fallen over myself to be fair. I don't know who's been speaking to you, but they'll tell you: everybody'll tell you I've been very reasonable. I've no questioned his command.' He gave a violent shake of his head. 'I haven't. But I could have, Mary. I'm no bragging when I say that. Anyone'll tell you who'd be in command of the Battalion if we went into battle tomorrow. Aye. And he knows that bloody well. "Oh yes, Sinclair," he said, "tomorrow, I think. *Not* a good idea today: not on a Sunday," and away he blew. He's in a funk, Mary. He's windy. He is. And, by God, I'll let him know that the morn. He's bloody good reason to be in a funk. I'm telling you.'

Jock was sweating now and he wiped his brow with his sleeve. He gave a sigh and asked politely,

'Have you got a hanky?'

'Only a small one.'

'That'll give me a thrill.'

She clicked her teeth again, and he smiled.

'No. No. Honestly, Mary. It will. I'm a very simple man.'

She dug into her handbag, holding it in the softness of her lap and Jock forgot about the Colonel's interview. He was still not satisfied that he had said all that was to be said, but he was a little happier. She gave him a handkerchief and he mopped his neck with it.

'I guess he's in a wee bit of a panic. But he's asked for it,' he said. She nodded, and he came back to her. Then he leant forward to fill his glass.

'I'll pay you for this whisky.'

'Of course you won't.'

'Aye, I will.'

'I wouldn't let you.'

'You used to let me.'

'That seems a long time ago.' She turned to put a record on the gramophone on the table by the side of the sofa.

'Och, we don't want that thing.'

'I've got some new records,' she replied, 'if you're wanting to be amused.' She placed the needle on the record and as she did this he leant forward and put a hand on her knee, just under her skirt. She did not turn round to push him away. She was trying to close the lid of the machine and she just said, 'Definitely no.'

'Och, Mary.'

'No.'

'You didn't used to say no. D'you remember that? Or have you conveniently'—Jock took long words very slowly—'have you conveniently forgotten?'

'You didn't used to be a stranger.'

'Mary, I'm back.'

'And stinking,' she said patiently. 'You left stinking and you've come back stinking. You can't turn the clock back, Jock.'

'You can begin again. Come on.'

'If you're not going to sleep I think you'd better take yourself a walk round the town.'

Jock smiled suddenly.

'I could make you if I wanted to,' he said gently. And she was immediately angry.

'Jock Sinclair, you're the most conceited man I've ever met. You're not all that great shakes. And there's lots that know that, I can assure you.' She added the last sentence quietly, and the noise of the record drowned it.

'What d'you say?' Jock asked and he shook his fingers at the gramophone. 'For Christ's sake put that thing off.'

'No.'

'You put it off, you besom.' He leant across her and tried to open the lid of the gramophone.

'No!' she said again and she tried to push him back but he was already drunk enough to be determined and he lunged forward. Clumsily he pushed the machine and it slipped off the coffee-table on which it rested, and fell to the floor. The needle made a loud noise as it scored the record. Then there was silence. Mary said nothing. She brought her lips closely together and leant back as he sat up again. He left one hand on her thigh and he gave an uncertain half smile.

'That's mucked it.'

She took him by the wrist, and pushed his hand away, then stood up to try and repair the damage.

'I don't know what the hell's the matter with you,' she said as they put the gramophone back on the table.

'What d'you mean?'

'This Colonel's really touched you.'

'What you say? Eh? That's a bloody lie. I've never felt better.'

'All right, all right,' she said, patient again, but Jock was not so easily appeased. He was standing up and he pulled his stomach up into his chest. He braced his shoulders.

'I've had a drink maybe. But there's nothing the matter. I've never been better. Christ, but you're a bloody woman.' He was inarticulate with irritation. He fidgeted, and clenched his fists. Then he drank half a tumbler of whisky in a gulp and he walked about the room. It was a moment or two before he spoke again, in a pleading tone.

'Och, Mary, I didn't come round to have a row. You know bloody well what the matter with us is . . . Why don't we get on with it?'

'Jock, you couldn't even manage now.'

'I could.'

She sighed, and shook her head.

'Och, anyway we could just sleep and that would be something,' he said.

'Oh dear, oh dear.'

'And I'll tell you what.' As the plan formed in his mind he took another gulp of his whisky. More in self-defence than anything else, she pushed the bottle towards him and he sat down again. 'We'll away out tonight, just like the old days. We'll be the *bona fide* travellers. That's how it'll be. It'll be the Highlander and the Red Lion, the Glasgow Bar and the Station.'

Mary was not the one to see a bottle of whisky go down someone else's throat, but she looked none the worse for wear herself. As she put the bottle down she said, 'It would be cheaper at your house.'

Jock turned away. 'I don't drink there.'

'Why ever not?'

'Morag, of course. You know fine. Stop getting at me. I'm no the man to drink in front of my daughter.' He waved his hand. 'We'll go round the publics. . . . Look, you'll let me pay for this bottle?' He reached in his wallet.

'You can put your money away.'

'No.'

'I'm all right for money.'

Jock hesitated. 'You're sure, lassie?'

'Sure and I'm sure.'

'And that dress suits you too.'

But soon after that Jock put his finger in his ear and shook his head. He was tiring a little.

'I'm sorry you weren't there this morning. You should have seen his face. And the other night. You know he was near greetin'.'

Not very long after, she saw that it would be impossible for him to leave. The excitement had worn off his cheeks and he grew drowsier and more apologetic.

At last she told him, when he seemed determined to go, that he should stay.

'You can't go. Not in your uniform: for heaven's sake. Away you go next door and sleep it off.'

Jock smiled meekly. 'You'll come too.'

'I'll pull the quilt over you.'

'You're a good girl.'

'There's no use fumbling, Jock,' she said patiently. 'Please.'

'Oh, Christ! Och Mary, I shouldn't have come. That's the truth of it. I thought you'd be pleased to see me. I shouldn't have come.'

'It's no matter. Come on now laddie, and we'll cover you up.'

'You're my bloody cherry-cake,' he said.

'Come away now: come on.'

When she heard him shouting, Mary ran through to the bedroom. Jock was shouting her name out loud. There was no overhead light in the room and she had to stumble as far as the bedside light while he still shouted. He was sitting bolt upright in the bed and he seemed to be in the throes of a fever: in spite of the chill of the room, his face and neck were covered with sweat, and his shirt was wet. Even when the light was switched on he kept shouting.

She stood back and said, 'Was it me you were calling?' She was groomed all ready to leave for some party, and she looked neat and efficient.

He mopped his brow and his cheek with the hard palm of his hand.

'Aye. It was either you or the Mother of God.'

'You nearly shouted the walls down. Are you sober, now?' Jock opened and closed his mouth once or twice.

'I've got a mouth like a parrot's cage.'

'That doesn't surprise me. It's time you gave up whisky, and that's a fact.'

Jock had grown used to the light now and he swung his legs over the side of the low bed. At some stage he had taken off his kilt and his stockings had dropped to his ankles; the red garters trailed loose round his feet. As he pulled up his stockings Mary noticed that he had climbed between the sheets.

'You'd no need to get between the sheets,' she said a little sourly, but Jock did not listen to her. He still looked half stunned, as if he were trying to remember something.

'What's the time?'

'It's twenty-five to eight. I'm off to supper in another five minutes.'

'Aye. Good for you.' He walked over to the radiator by the

curtained window, and picking up the towel there he wiped his neck with it. Then he shivered. The room was very cold and untidy, and nobody likes waking when it is dark.

'That's bloody strange, Mary. I was having some sort of dream.'

'It sounded more like a nightmare.'

'A-huh,' he said gently: he wanted to talk. 'That's what's so strange. Christ, I've been sweating.' He chucked the towel over the back of a chair and ran his fingers through his hair. His eyes were much brighter than usual: they did not look flat any more. 'I'm thinking it wasn't so bad. The dream wasn't so bad. No.'

'Well, you were fairly yelling for me. Here's your kilt. I was thinking of waking you up, anyway, when you started to cry.'

'I wasn't crying.'

'Then it was something very near it.'

'I'd no call to cry, lass. The whole Battalion was on the move.'

But Mary was too busy to listen to dreams.

'Here; take your kilt. I'll be through next door.'

She turned away, but as Jock sat down on the bed again he wanted her to stay.

'Mary, Mary, bide,' he said and she hesitated. 'It was a good dream. I was telling you.'

'Och, for heaven's sake, Jock.'

He gave a little smile. 'I was only wanting to tell you.'

'All right; all right. I'm glad it was a good dream. But it's time you were awake, and out of here.'

'That's the way of it?'

'Och.'

'Hi, Mary. What's the time?'

'I told you.'

'Did you?'

'It's after half-past seven.'

'Ach, to hell. I'm too late for the Mess.'

'Then you'd better go home.' She was standing holding on to the door, half in the room and half out. Jock was as anxious as a child that she should stay.

'I told Morag I'd be out.'

'She'll give you a boiled egg, I'm sure.'

'A-huh.' He smiled and bent down stiffly to collect his shoes. 'I'm no much good at amusing us, so it seems.'

'So it seems.'

Then Jock returned to the dream. 'I can't just mind what the hell it was all about. But it wasn't a nightmare: not really. It's cold, Mary. Is it snowing?'

She knocked her knuckles against the door with impatience.

'How should I know? I haven't left the flat.'

'You would have been as well in bed beside me then.'

Again she was about to leave.

'Mary?'

'I've got company,' she said and Jock looked up from his laces.

'Who the hell?'

'It's all right: it's a friend of yours. Never mind about the bed: I'll make it later.'

Jock was not very grateful. 'If you make it at all,' he said.

Charlie Scott was lying on the sofa with his head tipped back on the arm, and he did not move when Jock came into the room. When Charlie sensed danger all that happened was that his movements were a little slower, and his speeches even shorter. He was known for that. There was a live newsreel taken of his company going into an attack during the Italian campaign and Charlie had been something of a star in it. As the smoke thickened and his men deployed along the line of tanks, a runner came up with some message. There is a wonderful picture of Charlie taken on the spot, and you see it repeated from time to time when they show old shots of battle. The runner has a long message which you do not hear, and Charlie listens to him. He nods, and brushes his big moustache: he does not look flurried or afraid. You hear his voice, with the tanks behind.

'Tell Mr McLaren from me,' he says, 'that he must bloody well bide his time.' The message, though never understood or explained, served as a catch phrase in the Battalion for some time after that. And it was the same calm, dumb expression that confronted Jock when he came into the room.

But Jock could not disguise his astonishment.

'Charlie Scott. What the hell are you doing here?'

Then he looked at Mary's back. She was bending over a table at the far end of the room, pouring out some drinks, and it was all suddenly plain.

'Bit worried about you. Thought you might have tottered along here, old boy.'

Jock looked at him hard, looked at Mary, and looked back at him again. He blinked; then he smiled.

'Aye. Old boy, old boy. And you're a bloody liar, Charlie Scott. But you're a bloody bad liar. I'll give you that.'

'No, Jock lad, I . . .'

'Och, it's no business of mine,' Jock said irritably, turning away, and now Mary put a tumbler in his hand. 'I was just surprised.'

As casually as she could, Mary said, 'Don't worry, Charlie; Jock always judges others by himself.' But Jock shook his head. She was as unconvincing as Charlie. He chuckled as he said, 'And I'm always right.'

'Here's to us,' Mary said; then she put her glass down on the bookshelf and disappeared into the bedroom.

Charlie sat up and he raised his glass with a flippant little jerk.

'Astonishing good luck.'

'Aye,' Jock said, and he took a gulp. When he noticed it was brandy he was drinking he made a sour face. 'I suppose the whisky's done. Was it your bottle, Charlie?'

'Lord, no.'

'I'll repay you, sometime.'

Charlie sat silently and Jock walked up and down the room for a moment or two, touching things. Then he glanced at the door, and stepped back to Charlie. He bent forward and spoke in a low voice.

'Charlie; you're a bloody idiot, man. It's time you got out and got yourself married. You can't go on like this all your life.'

It was just like that newsreel. Charlie's face was without expression. At last he said slowly, 'You must have had the hell of a dream,' and he took a sip of brandy, but he did not much like the taste of brandy, either.

Jock looked at him earnestly then he straightened his back

again, and he said, 'Aye; the hell of a dream.' He walked over to the chair in the corner and picked up his bonnet.

Charlie said, 'Sorry about all this.'

'A-huh.' Jock had not meant to say any more on the subject, but now he nodded to the bedroom door. 'Anyway the bed's warm for you.'

'Nothing's warm these days, Jock: nothing except the bathwater.'

'Aye, aye.'

It was only after he had closed the flat door behind him that Jock remembered Charlie's confession on the night the Colonel had arrived. He had said it was fresh water. But Jock did not feel very much like smiling. He was worried: worried first because it had been the sort of dream that leaves a man worried: worried because he should never have gone round to see her; worried because he had said what he had said to Charlie; and finally, but most immediately of all, worried because he should have said a lot more to Charlie. When Charlie had said that about the bathwater he should have had an answer, or thrown a drink in his face. The thought of the bath and the bathroom annoyed him particularly. It was not that he was particularly in need of Mary, or any other woman. He supposed it was just something he had missed. Presumably, amusing men did it in the bath.

He was just about to wander down the stairs when Mary appeared on the landing beside him.

'Jock.'

He was surprised to see her, and she smiled kindly. She quickly closed the door behind her and she touched his wrist.

'Jock, you're all right?'

He stared at her slowly: at her eyes, and the set of the eyes, and at her hair. She smiled anxiously.

'I shouldn't have been cross like that.'

He cocked his head on one side.

'I'm all right, lassie. Dinny fash yourself.'

'I'm glad.' She was almost like a mother, saying goodbye to a schoolboy son. She did not seem to know quite what to say, but she was anxious to say something. 'It's fine seeing you again.'

Jock smiled now and shook his head. 'Will I call back?'

'Of course. I'm always pleased to see you,' she said looking away, and Jock began to chuckle.

'Away you go back to Charlie. Charlie's a bloody stoat.'

'Och, Jock. . . .' There was his coarseness again.

'Aye, aye.' He touched her hand and started to walk downstairs.

Charlie did not move from his place on the sofa when she returned to the room, and poured herself a drink. At last he said with a silly smile, 'Touching farewell?' and she gave him a look.

'I don't know what's the matter with you all. It used to be amusing, in the old days.' She shrugged. 'Och to hell.'

'Jock's certainly changed,' he said at last, and she stopped and tapped her nails against the empty glass in her hand. She opened her eyes very wide, as if she were day-dreaming.

'And what's that supposed to mean?'

Charlie swung his legs off the sofa, put his glass on the floor.

'I reckon he's heading for some sort of crack-up.'

'Is he drinking an awful lot?'

'That's nothing new.'

She was dreaming again.

'He was in a funny state today, no mistake. He came in here like an eighteen-year-old. Then he just faded away.'

'Oh yep?'

She smiled warmly, and moved. 'Jock's a great man.'

Charlie twitched his moustache.

'Let's not go on about it,' he said rather quietly, 'old girl.'

She looked at him and she knew what she should say. She could have touched him, or joked him. She could have said, 'He hasn't your moustache' or 'I didn't know you cared.' She could have said, 'For heaven's sake.' There were lots of formulae which would have fitted, but she somehow did not feel inclined to apply them. So they just left it at that.

ELEVEN

The weather had changed for the worst. The snow lay two or three inches deep on the causeways and in the wynds, and it was still falling. But there was nothing sleety about it now: each flake was a feather and the flakes fell thickly, with a silent perseverance. Above the yellow street lamps it was pitch dark, and people abroad that night wondered what would happen were it never to cease to snow. No footsteps rang on the pavements, and even voices were muffled and lost in a white felt world that was lonely and eerie. Echoes were suffocated by the same snow that falls each year and that fell so long ago, when the first Jacobites, routed, savage and afraid, retreated, burning the villages as they came. The women then—their lips moving and their voices lost—the women and the children escaped from their houses into this same white winter, and waited, moaning. Snow in those parts is altogether different from the Christmas-card showers in the South. It is more serious and more sinister. Snow once meant suffering and poverty, and even starvation: it brought sorrow, not Christmas. The conditions have changed, the storm is no longer a danger; but the memory of something that was experienced generations before lingers like a superstition. Snow comes not as a friend.

And of all men Jock was the most superstitious. A flake or two fell on his eyebrows so that he pulled his bonnet over his eyes and turned up the collar of his coat. He did not wear one of the short greatcoats that fashionable field officers wear: he wore the regulation officer's greatcoat. It was long and the two rows of heavy brass buttons ran parallel up to the waist, then flung apart from each other, wider and wider, so that the top buttons were shoulder breadth and the lapels folded across the chest.

He walked down Seaton Street, across the corner of the

park to the footbridge. Its surface is cobbled and as it is
steeply humped he found it difficult to walk there without
slipping. But at the crest he stopped in one of the bays in
the stone walls and leant over to look at the black water
swirling beneath. By the light of a single lamp he could see
where the snow was lying on a foot or two of ice that curved
in from the bank of the stream. And although there was
nothing heroic about Jock's face, the figure standing there
in the long greatcoat had a splendour. The same figure had
moved from platoon to platoon when the snow was falling
on a flatter, duller land: in every war, back and back, in
every siege and trouble that same figure existed and exists:
the anonymous commander in the long coat moving through
the night, alone. He is the guard.

Anxious, because it was a time for anxiety, he walked
on towards his home, to see Morag. He always felt a little
guilty when he returned from visiting Mary, but when he
found the house empty, he stopped still in the hall, suddenly
convinced that something was wrong. He reached out a hand
and touched the coat-stand, then took a pace forward to
switch on the lights.

'Morag! Morag! Morag!'

He glanced behind him, as always when afraid, and seeing
the door ajar, closed it with a brave bang. Then he went
swiftly to the kitchen, and finding it neat and orderly, tidy
and cleaned, with a little note propped up on a cup on the
bare table, his shoulders dropped with relief, and he opened
his coat with a smile of shame. The note read:

Father,

   Gone out with Jenny. Back by eleven.

                                                Morag.

It was written in a sane and slanting script, and was
firmly underlined. Jenny was a neighbour, and a friend of
Morag's. Nothing could be more secure. Jock looked about
the kitchen, and the larder. He looked in a tin and ate a
biscuit, then he knew he could not bring himself to make
some supper, so he buttoned his coat again, shoved his hands
deep into his pockets and retraced his steps down the wynd
over the bridge and back into the town. He decided to call
into a small hotel which had long ago been one of his haunts.

but which he had not visited for a full year. In the hall he was about to sign the book on the table as a *bona fide* traveller—between London and Thurso—when the proprietor appeared, ferret-like and inquisitive.

'Eh, Colonel Sinclair?'

Jock had never liked the man.

'Eh, you're travelling are you, Colonel?'

'I am.'

The proprietor pushed his face into the book. 'Eh, is this right?'

'Aye, it's right.'

'You've come fr' London?'

'No,' Jock said solemnly. 'From Thurso.'

'Dear me, Colonel . . . ,' the proprietor began.

'It says so there doesn't it, for Christ's sake?'

'I'm only doing my duty, Colonel Sinclair.'

The man fidgeted defensively. He was nervous of Jock. 'It's no right you should come in if you're no a *bona fide*.'

Jock spluttered. He had always thought it a stupid law and he had no intention of taking it seriously.

'For Christ's sake, all the law says is that we've got to sign the book. That's all you've got to carp about. All right?'

'Colonel, it's important that . . .'

'Well I've signed the bloody thing. O.K.?'

'There's still a question.'

'There's no question. I've signed it, haven't I?'

'Aye, you have that, Colonel.'

'Well for Christ's sake get out of my way.'

Jock clenched and unclenched his fists as he pushed open the inner door, with his shoulder.

The pub was patronized almost exclusively by the more senior members of the band. No piper would dare to go to the private bar until he was invited there, and after that first invitation he would hardly ever go to any other pub. Not that there was anything special in the way of entertainment. An upright piano was as much as it boasted. But business had been good and since Jock had last called the room had been redecorated, in brown and cream, and it had been filled with new furniture in the shape of pink and green wickerwork chairs and round glass-covered tables. The proprietor had

bought these at the sale of a seaside hotel the other side of
Portobello. But the bar itself had not changed: it still had
the coloured glass screen protecting it from the open part
of the house—the public bar, and the saloon. A sergeant
was stooping to order two beers and whisky chasers and he
grinned, rather embarrassed, in reply to Jock's nod.

Jock himself ordered a whisky from the waiter, and not just
a wee one; but it was a whisky that was never to be drunk.
As he started to unbutton his coat again he glanced round the
room and observed that there were five or six pipers there,
mostly non-commissioned officers, in their kilts and spats,
their sporrans swung round on their hips, all prepared and
all dressed up to get drunk. From the corner of his eye he
was surprised to see that there was a dark girl with a pale
face in the lounge: there were not often ladies present. Then
perhaps almost instantaneously—but this realization was
characteristic of the movements that followed, in that it
seemed to him a long time before he understood—he
saw that the piper with the girl was Corporal Fraser. He
also looked pale and he was rising to his feet, seemingly
disturbed. A second glance lasted for a split second, but
the picture was so firmly impressed on Jock's mind that it
seemed ever afterwards to have lasted for minutes. Morag
was sitting with her hands on the table: she was very
tense, and pale and her fingertips were pressing on the
glass. She put her hand out to hold Corporal Fraser back
for she must have known then what was going to happen.
Jock advanced on them. With anger, with that blind rage
that is always born of fear, he drew back his right hand,
and his fist was only half closed as if he were holding a big
stick. Then with a back-handed downward blow he struck
the Corporal, just as he was finding his voice to give an
explanation. Morag's fingers went up to her lips, and she
gave a whimper rather than a cry. The Corporal knocked
against the table and upset the glasses. Everybody in the
room stood up, uncertain whether to interfere or to hold
back, and Jock's voice came clear: 'You bastard'—with
the same short *a*, but no joke for Charlie this time, 'You
bastard . . .'

He would have struck the Corporal again, this time with a

closed fist, and Morag had already given out a warning cry, when a voice behind him called out sharply:

'Colonel Sinclair.'

It was Mr McLean, standing absolutely still, just inside the door. Jock turned and saw him, and came to his senses. With a sinking agony he saw what he had done and his jaw dropped, his face blank like a man awakened to the sound of guns. Suddenly all was noise around him. Chairs and tables were pushed about, the proprietor was there, somebody was looking at the Corporal's eye and Morag was in front of him whiter still, crying, 'I'm ashamed, I'm ashamed.'

He must have said something, protested, demanded; but it was the Pipe-Major who was in command and Morag went home to his house. When an officer strikes a ranker it is time for someone else to take command. The others paid up, moved out, gathered coats and chattels like citizens alarmed by war, and Jock found himself sitting in a chair with a stern-faced proprietor telling him to pull himself together and away out of here. The proprietor's face had a lot of lines on it and he looked like a lawyer's senior clerk; like that, or like a wolf.

'Away out o' here: I'm no having carryings on in this house. You must be out o' your senses. And still with your bonnet on.'

Jock nodded, and nodded, and the proprietor disappeared. He sat motionless for a few minutes, stunned by it all, appalled by what he had done, by what one blow had cost him, alone in a nightmare silence that was like the long high notes of a lament.

BOOK TWO

The Beating of Retreat

The dawn was like an afternoon; the day seemed to break with an immense regret. There were no bright streaks dramatic enough for an execution; but it was a prisoner's day, dull and without birds.

It was just freezing outside and the barracks was at its worst. The high wall closed out the real world like a frame surrounding an etching. A tint of brown in the sandstone was the only colour within the perimeter, apart from the white of the snow, and the grey: the grey of the slates where the snow had thawed a little and shifted in an untidy avalanche; the grey shoulders of the Officers' Mess at the end of the square; the grey figures scuttling about from block to block, the orderly corporals, the pickets dismissing, the bugler in search of breakfast, and the detention squads sweeping away the first paths through the sticky snow.

And in the middle of it all was another grey form, apparently in no hurry, walking clumsily, his head and shoulders wagging from side to side, like a great bear in a ring. Jock had not been to bed at all, and now he felt cold and sick. His feet were wet, every limb was dead-weight, every joint stiff, and his chin rested on his chest. Only once or twice did he look up. He stared blankly at the buildings and the figures moving about as the day began, he observed the lights going on in the barrack rooms, heard the echoes of the first complaints. He turned all the way round to look at every building, at the chimneys, and at the arc of sky. Two or three times he had hesitated and slightly changed his direction; he left a track of his indecision behind him in the snow. Then he lifted his head and marched towards the stucco villas of the Married Quarters (Warrant Officers and non-commissioned ranks). These were hidden behind the Officers' Mess in the northernmost part of the area, and every house was dismally identical.

Jock expected Morag to come into the cramped little room. He was sitting like a bundle in a greatcoat, heaped into a modern armchair. Mrs McLean's parlour was very spick-and-span with its tiled fireplace, piano, antimacassars, calendars, and obstacles galore. If the furniture was displaced by six inches in any direction, there was no thoroughfare from the window to the fire or to the door. Jock stood up awkwardly when he heard the approaching footsteps, and the Pipe-Major nodded to him.

'I'd thought she would come down, but she's very determined.'

'Did you tell her it was me?'

'Yes, sir.'

'Did you tell her the rest? What I said you'd to say?'

'Aye. Mrs McLean and I have both had a word with her.'

'And what did she say?'

'She said she was tired.' He gave a gesture of sympathy. 'The lassie's worn out: that's all it is.'

Slowly, slowly Jock picked his way through the furniture to the little space in the bow of the window. He was careful that the borders of his coat should not sweep away any ash-tray or ornaments and he still had hold of the cloth when he replied cautiously, 'But I said I apologized.' His hands came away from his coat. The light shone on the upturned palms. 'I said I was sorry. Does the lassie think it was easy for me? Does she suppose it doesn't cost me anything to say that? What more could I say?'

Mr McLean shook his head. He was at a loss, and he was afraid of Jock; afraid that Jock might fail.

Outside it had already begun to thaw. Some snow had slipped off the roof and there were a few drops of water falling from the rone pipe outside the window. There was some moisture on the window itself: just enough to tempt Jock to draw a double cross with his finger and rub it out again with the side of his fist. He left his fist resting on the pane and stared and stared at the greyness outside.

Mr McLean shifted uneasily and ran his fingers up and down the leather strap of his sporran. He smiled.

'Och, Colonel Sinclair, you know what the young girls are. You know what the daughters are like: she'll come away. She's upset. It's her dignity that's suffered. It is her pride.'

Jock moved at 'pride'.

'A-huh. It's her pride.' He seemed too tired to go further than that and he dug his hands in his coat pockets. Then he smiled, moving his hands in the pockets with a sort of shrug.

'It's like having your own words flung back in your face. I taught her to be proud, Pipe-Major. I taught her independence. Christ, I don't know why I bothered sending her to school. I taught her everything she knows.'

'She's a fine girl. But she's like yourself. That is all that is the matter. She will come away. She is still upset: and the lassie is tired.' His voice fell softly, like truth. But Jock's was grating:

'Ach, I should have known she would not come downstairs. She's ashamed of me. I shouldn't have come—and that's a fact.' He nodded and recovered himself. 'It's good of you to look after her.'

Again he stood still, and there was another silence. Then at last Mr McLean frowned and he said, 'I cannot understand it. I cannot follow.' He put his hand out in front of him as if he were groping for a solution. 'A man of your experience; to do such a thing. Such a stupid thing. You can't have considered.'

Jock stared at him, but did not reply.

'It was a terrible thing,' the Pipe-Major said and he sat down on the arm of the chair. Jock pulled a cigarette packet from his pocket. It was squashed, and there was only one cigarette in it. He rolled the cigarette round his fingers, reshaping it, and tapped the tobacco in at the ends. He lit it with a match from the other pocket, and he smoked, and sniffed. He seemed unwilling to go on or to go back; just as if he were idling; a soldier on a field, waiting to be taken away.

'What d'you think made me do it?'

The Pipe-Major hesitated, nodding here and there with his head.

'Man to man, Mr McLean. Forget the badge of rank. It can be forgotten now.'

The other protested. 'Oh no, sir, it's no as bad . . .'

Jock raised his hand.

'Man to man.' He sat back on the window seat, his coat ruffled about him, his knees apart. 'What are you thinking?'

'You didn't know about the young man?'

'No.'

The Pipe-Major raised his head again. 'She didn't tell you?'

'No.'

'Maybe it was a shock. Just that.'

'A-huh.' Jock looked out of the window, idle again.

And at last the Pipe-Major spoke out: 'I know he's a corporal, sir: but he's a good lad. He's no a fly-by-night, Ian Fraser. His father's a farmer up by Forres there.'

Jock moaned and he pushed his legs out in front of him. His heels clicked on the floor, and he shook his head backwards and forwards as he tried to find words.

'Did you think that? Och, man. . . . For Christ's sake. I expected Mr Simpson to say that—not you. I expected every old school tie from here to St. James's Palace to say that. . . .' He shook his head again, clicked his fingers to correct himself. 'That's not right either. I expected half of them to say just "You know Jock—a ranker born, a ranker aye"; and the others I expected to say what you're saying. I mean the complex boys. The doctor with his fingers tangled in his hair. "Jock's self-made," he'll say, only he'll say it with a lot of whys and wherefores, and "should have thoughts" and "in effects" and all that caper.'

The Pipe-Major was a little mystified. He frowned as he tried to follow and Jock rambled on.

'"It's no wonder Jock was so upset when he saw his lassie with a corporal." Ach. To hell. I've never had time, Mr McLean, I've never had time to get as complicated as that. I leave all that to the county.' For the first time that morning a twinkle of humour lit his eyes. 'I've been most things, Mr McLean, but I've never been a Regimental Sergeant-Major.'

The Pipe-Major understood and smiled, then Jock went on.

'Nach, nach. To hell with that. Whatever they may like to believe I've never had any worries about class. Aye, and I'm sorry. It hurts me that you should think that of me.' Then he added, 'And me a piper, too.'

Jock's intelligence was never to be underestimated. Whether he thought out the moves, and played the game accordingly, or whether the outburst was spontaneous, the Pipe-Major did not stop to think. But his words could not have fallen on more sympathetic ears. Mr McLean, even so early in the morning, began to glow, and to nod. His eyes glistened with favour.

'Aye, sir, and I hold the same views as you do, though they being so near the politics it's no my job to express them. I'm glad of what you've said to me. If it had been the other way I couldn't have felt the same at all. We have no place for class here in a Highland Regiment. No place at all. But we're as well disciplined as the next, are we not?'

The Pipe-Major was throbbing with enthusiasm, and Jock glanced at him slantwise. His eyes were moving quicker now. He was on his feet again, twisting and gesturing.

'Mr McLean, you've been with the Battalion a while.'

'Seventeen years, sir.'

'Aye. All through the war.'

'I didn't miss any of it.'

'You were hurt, once?'

'Aye. On the great day. I was playing then. I was piping when you took over command.' He allowed himself a moment of pride. 'And I still played when they took me back and bound up my leg.'

'Aye, I remember.' Jock paused and they both remembered the day. Then Jock spoke again. 'They were the days of my glory, Mr McLean. Nobody can deny me that. They were the days of my glory,' he said with wily tragedy.

'Nobody would ever want to deny you those days.' Mr McLean clenched his jaw with the sort of vigour that usually takes whisky. He was not usually boisterous in his loyalty, but this was an exceptional moment. 'Not any piper anyway. I'll see to that.'

'Even if I strike him?' Jock looked up suddenly, his eyes pale.

Mr McLean was about to answer warmly again. But he hesitated when he saw where the conversation had led him, and he was ashamed that he could not answer straight. He let his head drop and put two fists on his knees.

'Colonel Sinclair. Colonel Sinclair.'

Jock gave a weary smile. 'Och, never mind.' He rose to his feet, preparing to leave, and Mr McLean talked fast and anxiously.

'It's not an important thing. It will come out that it's not an important thing. It is a pity; no more. Sir, if it were only Corporal Fraser and myself there'd be no need . . . but you must see. There were others there. There was the landlord and the other pipers. It is not possible to ignore it. It would not be right for me. I cannot forget it. But it will soon blow away.'

Jock shook his head.

'It'll go to court martial.'

'The Colonel could deal with it.'

'The Colonel will put it to Brigade. It will go to court martial.'

The Pipe-Major sighed. He knew very well that was the truth. He smiled sadly.

'I wish I had a television set. I've never wished it before. But if I had a television set perhaps I would not have gone out at all.' He grew serious again. 'At the court martial they will see that it is not important. Then it will be forgotten.'

Jock shook his head again.

'You know very well that if it goes as far as court martial, whatever the result, it is the end for me.'

'No, no. It'll be forgotten. They wouldn't demote you on that.'

Jock looked at him steadily.

'H.Q. Company Commander until they axe me. For Christ's sake.'

Mr McLean fidgeted, and Jock went on, heatedly this time. 'Man, the Battalion belongs to me; without it, there's nothing else for me. D'you know that?'

'I know that.'

'If it goes to court martial, it will be the finish.'

The Pipe-Major grew agitated: 'Colonel Sinclair. You are

making it hard for me. It is my duty. No one could be more sorry than myself. Colonel Sinclair, I tell you, I'd walk the plank for you.'

'Would you?' He paused, then he moved away and he said, 'Ach!'

He was suddenly unreasonably angry with the man. Mr McLean seemed to him too resilient to be human, a man sitting on his haunches, riding every punch. His eyes blazed up, he moved, suddenly, pushing his way through the furniture.

'And tell me this; if there's war tomorrow, who's leading the Battalion? Eh?'

The Pipe-Major was hurt. He remained silent, and Jock passed him, saying, 'Och, to hell with this.'

But in the hall as he reached for his bonnet, he practically stumbled into Morag, who had come downstairs, thinking he was gone. She drew back and she saw his hair tousled, the creases in his coat, the soaking wet shoes and stockings. These were things Morag had grown used to observing. Even though she was afraid to meet him, and determined to draw stiffly away from him, she could not hold back.

'Father, for heaven's sake. . . .'

There was a note of sympathy in the voice, and such a note, however slight, is impossible to miss. Jock could not have failed to hear it. But he looked at her with pale, flat eyes as if he were defending himself: as if she had spoken in another tongue.

'Ach!' It was a noise, not a word, and Morag drew her elbows into her sides.

'Father, you're soaked through.'

He shook and turned away. In a rough voice, with a drunkard's brutality, he said, 'Och, you can keep all that stuff. You wrote me a lie and you're too bloody late now,' and before she moved, he hurled himself out of the front door, slamming it hard behind him. He walked heels down, determinedly through the snow, with obstinacy in every stride. After only a moment he was miserable but he knew he could not return to the house; his obstinacy prevented that.

TWO

An hour later Jimmy Cairns saw Jock, and by then a great deal had happened.

When Jimmy arrived at Battalion H.Q. that Monday morning there was already a buzz in the air. A filing clerk was leaving the Colonel's room, and Mr Simpson had just re-entered. The Colonel himself was in a fever of excitement. His hands were on his hips, his eyes were bright and he was lighter than ever, lighter than thistledown, perpetually on tiptoe. He was like a politician flitting house, sending people here and there, talking on the telephone, jotting down notes on a pad. Nobody knew exactly what was happening. Everybody made a guess. All this Jimmy saw from his own office as his assistant dashed in and out, but it was a little while before he picked up the first scents of the story. The key seemed to lie in the doctor's visit. Barrow and he had spent half an hour closeted together and it was known now that the doctor had been called across to the Band Block because a piper had been hurt. From one of the sergeants in the office, from a brief talk with Mr Riddick, and from the hush-hush expression on Simpson's face, Jimmy managed to piece the story together. Then he was called in himself. Barrow made an effort to look grave, but he could not stand still. He bounced about the room as he said how serious and awkward was the situation.

'I have reason to believe—no evidence, you understand, Jimmy, but reason to believe that a corporal was struck by an officer in a bar last night.'

Jimmy nodded, and Barrow continued.

'Well, well,' he clipped his words, in this mood. 'Of course we must take steps.'

'Sir. Have you rung the proprietor?'

Barrow smiled. 'No evidence there. The men shouldn't

have been given drinks anyway. He won't make any statement. If the newspapers got hold of the story he'd lose his
seven-day licence. He might lose his licence altogether. No
. . . no. The evidence lies within the barracks. There were
other people there. We could get some sort of a story but
it's a question of whether we want to go so far.'

Barrow bounced over the other side of the room and
flapped a piece of paper that was pinned on a board there.

'Whether we want to go on,' he said again, with a little
drama. 'It would probably be a court martial, you know.' He
shook his head. 'That sort of thing doesn't do the Battalion's
name any good.'

'It does its name more harm if the story leaks out and we
do nothing about it.'

'You think so?' Barrow opened his eyes wide: he looked
curiously innocent. But Jimmy did not have a doubt.

'Of course.'

Barrow nodded, and he steadied a little.

'It's very difficult.'

'So,' Jimmy often said when he did not quite understand.

'The personalities in the case complicate things. I've called
for Charlie Scott. We'll talk it over, the three of us.'

'So.'

Almost in passing Barrow said, 'Jock's involved,' and at
last it all made sense to Jimmy. He understood the buzz now,
and the Colonel's fidgeting. The game had fallen into his
hands. As the situation dawned on Jimmy he began to look
sad. He did not enjoy the look in Barrow's eye: he did not
quite believe in the anxious expression. He almost felt that
Barrow was cheating. But Jimmy could not have explained
these things even to himself. He just had a feeling that way,
but his distaste showed clearly in his expression. Meantime
Barrow rested on his heels.

'A very unpleasant business. And, as you can appreciate,
awkward. My motives are bound to be suspected. Then
that's neither here nor there.' He was anxious to talk: the
words came fast. 'Clearly I can't be expected to take a purely
objective view of the thing. That's why I've asked Scott to
come along. It's all a great pity.'

'Jock never struck a corporal,' Jimmy said slowly.

'Well, yes . . . I'm afraid he did. There's really not much question about it.' He went into a few details. The doctor had picked up a great deal of information. He knew Morag was staying over in the Married Quarters.

'All that proves nothing. It's no business of the doctor's either,' Jimmy said. 'He's always talking.'

'Jimmy, five minutes ago I received a request from Mr McLean that I should see him as soon as possible.' He handed over a piece of paper on which the formal request was made. *I remain, Sir, your obedient servant.*

'So,' Jimmy said again, and he was prepared to wait until Charlie came round. But he did not get the chance of seeing Charlie before they saw the Colonel. Barrow was too good a tactician. He kept Jimmy with him until Charlie arrived. He invented one reason after another to keep him in the office. Barrow's mind seemed to be working five times faster than ever before. He was planning fast: interviews ahead.

And when Charlie came things did not go at all as Jimmy had expected. There was no long discussion. All the pros and the cons were not trundled out. Indeed the preliminaries to the interview were as long as the main discussion itself. Barrow was at his most tortuous. He had a habit of discussing general political news, perhaps because he always knew more of current affairs than any of his colleagues. For the most part the officers lived body and soul within the limits of the high wall; Macmillan could gossip a little on social items, but even he was inclined to concentrate on county news. Some of the other more earnest officers knew something of the disturbances in other parts of the globe, Malaya, Kenya or Korea, because they had friends there, but by and large they were innocent of world, and even of national, affairs. Something had evidently been happening in the United States: it had to do with Communism. There was some scandal about a trial on television. Barrow made reference to it, described it, and condemned it. That took a moment or two and gave time for Charlie to sit back in his chair and stretch out his long legs. He laid his crook beside them. Charlie always carried his crook, rather than the regulation ash walking-stick.

Jimmy sat on the edge of his chair, impatient of the

preliminaries, and he looked hard at Charlie while Barrow outlined the reason for their meeting. To give him his due he put the matter very fairly. He did not ask for a decision until he had mentioned Jock's name. He could almost certainly have won a tactical point by asking for Charlie's decision on the basis of the accused being an anonymous officer. But he did not try any tricks, and he added, too, that all he wanted now was Charlie's opinion. The decision must rest with him, and the only question at this stage was whether a formal enquiry should be conducted. Depending on the results of this independent enquiry a report would or would not go up to Brigade, putting the question of court martial. It was a very fair statement, and Barrow was at his best, a barrister in command of his brief. He seemed much concerned: seemed very sincere. He did not add an unnecessary word.

Charlie stroked his moustache, then he pouted.

'Well there's no doubt about it, is there?'

'Please?' The lines about Barrow's eyes grew deeper in his anxiety.

Charlie gave a shrug. 'Well, of course you've got to make an enquiry. We can't have chaps poking corporals in the eye, after all.'

Jimmy's fingers came together: he pitched forward in the low chair. He was so upset by Charlie's reaction that it took him a moment or two to find words to express himself, even inadequately. He stuttered and made a false start. Then he came back again.

'Charlie . . . of course we know that, but Jock . . . hell, it's different. Jock's always had his own methods.' He stopped, and twisted. 'Och. He must have had reason. If the Corporal was to put in a complaint it might be different, but you know what they are with regards to Jock up at Brigade. A thing like this would kill him. It's dynamite. Surely the way to do it is for the Colonel here to have a word with him. . . .' Jimmy looked from one to the other. Barrow's face was a blank. He stared hard at Charlie who was staring at his toes. Barrow said nothing; he just stared at Charlie with a strange amazement. At last Charlie lifted heavy eyelids and rested his baleful eyes on Jimmy.

''Fraid I can't agree, old man,' he said, and Jimmy felt cold.

'But, Charlie . . .'

He was interrupted there. Charlie clambered to his feet, addressing Barrow. ''Course, it's your decision.'

'Of course,' Barrow nodded, recovering himself.

'It won't make you very popular, I'm afraid.'

Barrow gave a stiff nod.

'That's the fate of a C.O.,' he said bravely, and Charlie nodded. Jimmy was still groping about him, hopelessly, but the interview was already over.

'Not nice at all,' Charlie said, as he knocked along. He explained to Jimmy, at the door, that he had to trundle: there was some sort of kit inspection on that morning. But Jimmy would not let him go. He spoke almost in a whisper, and he made sure the door was closed behind him.

'Charlie, we can't let it go like this.'

Charlie shrugged.

'Charlie, we can't.'

'Old chum: we've been boiling up to this for some time. It isn't nice, but it's one of those things. Old Jock's on the rocky side. I wouldn't have been surprised if he'd brained the chap.'

'But it'll finish Jock: it'll fix him once and for all.'

'That is a pity.' Charlie drew himself up, and Jimmy looked down at his desk. Just before he went, Charlie said, 'Don't take it too hard, chum. I mean we've got to think of the Battalion sometimes. Have you ever seen such a shambles? That cocktail party, eh?'

'That was half Barrow's fault.'

Charlie smiled.

'That's quite another problem. But it's Jock who led us into this state when all's said and done. Did you see how he behaved over that dancing class? What? The old boy's a warrior and all that but, old chum, it's about time we had a colonel again, isn't it? And just a fragment of discipline. How can you look after the Rattrays when you've Jock at the top?'

'D'you think that? D'you really think that?'

'Yep. 'Fraid I do.'

Jimmy tapped his fingers on the desk. 'I've sometimes thought it,' he admitted, unwillingly.

'There you are. It's rough I suppose. And really I don't want to be involved. Couldn't want to less. But maybe some day someone'll put his nose over the barrack wall and really see what goes on. Then what? Eh? It's not going to be nice at all.'

Jimmy wavered. 'Maybe you're right there. But Jock— well he's different.'

'Don't let it give you ulcers, Jimmy. They'll do the same to you and me one day. I must be rolling. Bloody kit inspection. 'Bye.'

Simpson, now one move behind events, was anxious to talk things over with Jimmy but he got no further information, and at last he went on his way, leaving Jimmy pacing up and down his little office, biting his lip and scratching his hair.

A few moments later his train of thought was disturbed by noises in the lobby outside, and he recognized Jock's voice among them. He went out to discover Jock talking to Simpson and Mr Riddick.

Jock was still looking very crumpled, and if he had not been certain before, Jimmy was then certain of the truth of the story. It was written in every crease in Jock's clothes, in the hang of his coat: it was written straight across his face. Jimmy was shocked by the sight of him.

Jock nodded good-morning to him.

'Jimmy, what the hell's going on here?'

But Jimmy had still not had time to recover himself. Mr Riddick in twenty years of loud shouting had never lost his voice, and always with his seniors he had a glibness.

'Colonel Sinclair, sir, suggests the Commanding Officer ordered him here for interview this morning.'

Jock would never ordinarily have let Mr Riddick speak for him. He was the one man in the Battalion who could send him chasing: but he now made no complaint. He merely nodded and said, 'The other night after the cocktails.'

Mr Simpson, in his fortnight as Assistant Adjutant, had developed the manner of an aide-de-camp. Everything was difficult if it concerned Barrow. Barrow was always busy.

'The Colonel didn't mention it this morning. Perhaps he intended to see Colonel Sinclair later.'

Jimmy looked at him as if he were very far away, then he looked hard at Mr Riddick.

'I'll cope with this.' They moved, to go their separate ways. Jimmy looked at Jock and looked away again. 'There must have been some muck-up. Hang on a minute, Jock, if you will. I'll go and see him.' He touched Jock on the elbow as he passed him. Jock nodded gratefully, like a patient at a clinic, and he wandered into Jimmy's office and played with the inkpot on his desk while the other went next door to tackle Barrow. The sight of Jock fumbling with the inkpot touched Jimmy. He stared back at him through the doorway and he was suddenly ashamed and angry, both at once.

When Jimmy reminded him of the interview, Barrow rose from his seat and he said secretively:

'Close the door Jimmy; close the door.' And Jimmy wearily obeyed. 'Look, I'd forgotten this one. It's rather awkward. I don't want to see him now. D'you think he knows?'

Jimmy did not help. He looked hostile, and Barrow continued, 'D'you suppose he's gathered we're on to something?'

'I haven't the foggiest idea.'

Barrow nodded. He was upset by the idea of the interview, and he was fidgeting again, but this time not with impatience. He did not know which way to turn. He snatched at the air.

'I say, perhaps it might be an idea if you were to tell him that this business had come out, and it's clearly better that we didn't have a talk now. It wouldn't help. You needn't tell him I consulted Charlie and you. But put him in the picture.'

Jimmy was amazed. He took a step forward, and his head was held slightly to one side.

'Me, tell him, Colonel? *Me*?'

Barrow panicked a little. He fluttered. He looked back at Jimmy with eyes that had grown darker as his face grew pale. He gave a nervous little smile.

'I thought it might be more tactful.'

'Tactful!'

Another horrid little smile: Barrow cleared his throat.

'You don't think that's a good idea?'

'Colonel, for God's sake.'

'No. No, perhaps you're right. Yes, of course. It was only a passing idea. Stupid of me. It would place you in an awkward position. I tell you what. Later. Tell him I'll see him later.'

'What time?'

'Well, this afternoon.'

'He'll want a time.'

'Five-thirty? Rather late perhaps, but . . .'

'Five-thirty.' Jimmy turned, but Barrow spoke again before he opened the door.

'Jimmy, I say. I was rather surprised by Scott's reaction. What?'

'Yes, sir.'

'He's right, of course. Hadn't expected him to take such an objective view. Jimmy, we must take an objective view. That's essential. We can't take any side other than the Battalion's side. You see that?'

'I understand that.'

'I can assure you that's what guides me. That's true. The Battalion's side.'

'Yes, sir.'

Barrow's shoulders dropped. 'I say, I was thinking of nipping down to the Mess in ten minutes: get a cup of coffee. It's been quite a morning.'

Jimmy looked him straight in the eye, and without mercy. Barrow went on.

'Care to come?'

'I've a lot on hand, sir.'

'Oh.' Barrow moved nervously back to his desk. 'Of course. Righto. I'll only be gone fifteen minutes.'

'Colonel.'

THREE

A soldier does not most need a brain to think with, nor yet an arm to strike with; he needs teeth to hang on with, and Jock had those teeth. He went all the way back home, that same Monday morning, and he washed and shaved. He brushed his hair, he put on his best tunic, pulling it tight under his belt so it had no creases, he stared at himself in his mirror, saw to it that his teeth were clean and he said 'Resilience, boys, resilience.' He put clean stockings on, and adjusted the bright red flashes on his garters. He dusted his brogues and polished the badge in his bonnet and said, 'Aye, and we're dead but we won't lie down, come away then, come away.' He polished the buttons on his coat and turned the collar neatly down, he pulled his bonnet over his eye, then with a swagger and a bright dash he swung down to the bridge, across the park, back to barracks.

He must have understood that they all knew as soon as he put his big nose through the door of the ante-room soon after one o'clock. He twitched his nostrils and his eye roved round the room. Officers were huddled over beers and pink gins. They glanced up at him and mumbled 'good-morning' or nodded with studied normality. Barrow had gone into lunch, but most of them were there talking and smoking. Jock gave a little smile as he strode up the middle of the room to the big log fire. Turning his back to it, he lifted up the pleats of his kilt, to warm his bare bottom.

'A-huh,' he said, 'Dusty would you be so kind as to push that tit in the wall there, and we'll see if I can get myself a drink.'

When the waiter appeared with a tray in his hand, Jock shouted at him across the room.

'Good-morning, Corporal.'

'Morning, sir.'

Jock eyed him. 'You're feeling the heat, Corporal?'

The Corporal smiled uncertainly: the other officers were all watching now.

'It's cold, sir.'

'No wonder it's cold, lad. You're nude. Do up your collar button.'

'Sir.' The Corporal obeyed very quickly and Jock said:

'And you can bring me one hell of a whisky.'

'Sir.'

'Steady, steady; wait there, laddie. What are you drinking, Charlie?'

Charlie hesitated, 'Actually, thinking of lunch . . . you know . . .' he mumbled on.

'What are you drinking, eh? I'm asking something that's a question of fact.' Jock gave a little grin, and looked all round the room. 'Not just a rumour,' he said, and there was a little stir. 'What's in your hand?'

'Pink.'

'And one hell of a pink,' Jock gave the order.

'You, Jimmy?'

'Bottle of beer.'

Jock turned to the waiter again: 'And two bottles of beer in one can. C'mon, c'mon gents, make your orders. It's too cold a morning not to have something to drink . . . Well, well; and what's news today? Eh, is there no news?' His head on one side. 'Surely we've some bit of gossip, eh, MacKinnon?'

'It snowed,' MacKinnon said, rather frightened, and then he blushed. Jock gave a roar of laughter.

'Plus ten for observation, lad,' he said, but with a broad grin that would have made anything he said sound pleasant. It was as if the officers sitting there were tired members of some orchestra, and in the hands of the cleverest conductor. Slowly, with something less immediate than magnetism, more like a sort of suction, he was drawing life out of them. They all began to look up, and take notice. They stared at him as if it were the first time they had seen him; and perhaps more—as if it were the last time.

Jock had never looked so gallant since the days before the peace. He found his charm again that morning: his

eyes twinkled, and his hands moved with an eloquence.
Soon after, he was recalling the days when the Battalion
had been taken back for rest, shortly before the end of the
war. The officers had stayed for a while in a ridiculous Belgian
country house which still had great oil paintings on the wall,
but which was equipped with Naafi furniture. There they had
stayed until they dispersed for leave. Most of them had gone
as far as Brussels. Some had gone home. But Jock had stayed
there all the time, and when they had returned in ones and
twos, lonely and dejected, Jock had been there in front of the
fire, warming his celebrated bottom. The memory was only
vivid for one or two of them now: others were of an age to
have known it but they had been with some other Battalion at
the time, with the Second in the Far East, or on special duties,
or they had been prisoners. But they were all interested to
hear Jock speak of it, because he never spoke much of the
days of his glory. It would have been impossible for him to
recall truthfully one week of the campaign without sounding
now as if he were bragging, and something made him brag
about other things. They had all heard about his piping and
his boxing days, the days he had told the Sergeant-Major off,
and so on and on. But this was the very first time some of them
had heard him speak of the war, and he suddenly engulfed
them with the same charm that buoyed them all up in the
bad old days. Those that had been there remembered only
too vividly, and Jimmy looked quite upset. He had been a
platoon commander then, dressed up to be shot, and he came
back from his aunt in Crieff, taking two nights on the journey.
At three o'clock, burdened with kit and straps, he had shoved
his way into the hall of this house in Belgium. There, on a
red trolley with chrome wheels, two other subalterns were
tobogganing down the corridor. They greeted him with the
kind of sickeningly hearty welcome that athletes give you
when you are wrapped up in your overcoat, and Jimmy did
no more than nod and say as enthusiastically as he could that
he had enjoyed his leave. He wandered over to the table in a
spin of loneliness and there he found a letter from his sister
which had been written to him before he went on leave. He
knew about it; he knew what it said; he had seen her
since: but the pitch of his loneliness was such that he put

it in his pocket and gripped it hard as he went into the room which they called the ante-room, just for old times' sake. It was really the drawing-room.

Jock was sitting by the fire, eating a huge jam sandwich. He was alone in the room and he just gave a little flick of his head. He spoke quietly.

'Come away in, Jimmy lad, and I'll give you a jammy piece.' And he gave a great wide smile.

Jimmy suddenly could not stand it any more, as Jock recalled those days.

'Jock man, I've got to speak to you,' he interrupted, and the others looked round at him. Jock was in the middle of a description of one of the female cooks. His hands paused, and he looked up.

'What's that?'

Charlie frowned, but nothing could stop Jimmy now.

'Look, Jock . . . I've got to have a word with you.'

'A-huh. Well, what is it?'

'Not here,' Jimmy looked embarrassed.

'Is it shop?'

'Sort of. It's dead important, Jock.'

Jock looked slowly round the group; then he nodded towards Charlie, and stroking his upper lip as if he wore a moustache, just as Charlie had done in that ridiculous news film, he said, '"Then tell Mr McLaren from me, that he'll have to bide his time."'

Jock always laughed at his own jokes; but a catch phrase is irresistible. Jimmy was the only one who did not laugh. Even Charlie gave a funny, vain little twitch of his moustache.

'It's dead important, Jock,' Jimmy said again, but Jock shook his head: more than his head, his whole shoulders moved from side to side as if he had to roll to articulate.

'Jimmy, Jimmy lad: nothing's that important, nothing at all.'

Jimmy looked at the others. Charlie was leaning back, looking at his tumbler. Macmillan with a gesture of the long brown fingers said, 'It might be important; really quite.' Macmillan's nails were perfect.

'Christ knows what you boys think I am,' Jock said, smiling again; twinkling as he raised his glass to his lips. He held his glass between finger and thumb with the other fingers out in the air. 'Christ, you must think I'm deaf, dumb and blind.' He grinned. 'You're all bloody cheeldron. Now I was telling you about Lily . . .'

'Who's Lily?'

'Christ man, this cook I was going on about.'

'She was called Bella.'

'Dusty boy, you're losing grip of yourself. It was Lily.' Dusty shrugged. Jock very nearly insisted, then he too shrugged and he said, 'Well whatever she was called, she . . .' And away he went. There were more drinks, and everybody started talking louder. After a while even Jimmy seemed to have forgotten his frown in the flood of pleasant recollections. They were talking about the regimental orders then: the kit they used to walk about in—the jerkins, corduroys, peak caps, striped scarves. It would not have suited Douglas Jackson, so they had a laugh at his expense. Jock was speaking louder, but he still seemed mellow. But when the swing door squeaked and Barrow walked in from the dining room, the conversation died away. Barrow looked up nervously and he seemed to be about to make one of his famous 'Good-night all' remarks but Jock saved him. His voice had none of the usual challenge. It was perfectly sincere.

'Come and join us, Colonel.'

'Thank you.' But the Colonel was not flexible enough, nor his ear true enough; so he mistook the tone. 'Thank you; I've had lunch.'

'Well, have a cognac.'

He looked at Jock, then from one face to another. He seemed to want to join them but suddenly he decided to leave. 'I've got to shoot this afternoon. I won't, if you don't mind.'

'A-huh,' Jock said, disappointed, and he turned back to the others. Barrow paused, his weight on one foot. Again he looked as if he were going to say something: then very suddenly he turned away and left the room. In the hall, just outside the door, he paused, trying to listen. Then with a frown of self-condemnation he moved away.

He was not going shooting. That was another unnecessary lie. He seemed incapable of speaking the truth to Jock. He was almost like a son with a father too fierce: in order not to offend he told a half-truth, until the time came when he found it more natural to lie. It was perfectly obvious to him why he did this. Everything about Jock frightened him. His authority, his unpredictability, his bluntness. It was more than that. The very depth of his voice and the thickness of his forearm made Barrow afraid.

Jock never got into lunch at all, and that was a mistake. The others ate in ones and twos and returned to the ante-room to take their coffee with him, and he must have had more than half a bottle by then. But even Jock knew very well that he had drunk the charm away. He was much louder now, and bantering, and sarcastic. Every time he made a sarcastic remark he tried to withdraw it, laughing, shrugging, throwing his arms about and roaring, 'And away we go.'

When the telephone rang, MacKinnon, as Orderly Officer, went to the hall to answer it, and he returned to say that it was the exchange asking for the C.O. who was being called by Command at Edinburgh.

Jock insisted that he should answer it.

'Away we go then. Big Jock Sinclair'll have a word with the gentlemen in Edinburgh. For Christ's sake tuck your feet in or I'll fall on my neb.'

He pushed his way through chairs and tables, like a tank, and he opened the swing door by striking it with the palms of both hands at a level above his head.

His mood when he returned was one they all knew. As he addressed them, and they all kept very quiet, he fumbled with the coffee urn, the milk and the sugar. He rattled about the tray, looking for a spoon. He said nothing about the call for a moment, then he began:

'A-huh, Charlie. You're the lad for a crisis,' and Charlie's cheek muscle moved. He pushed his legs stiffly in front of him. Jock's head was turning and his eyes rolling as he brought them all into the act. 'Aye, aye. And you're the hell of a one for the women. Bloody good! Aye. I've always said it. The rest of us is just envious.'

'Jock, Jock, Jock.'

'Who's there? Eh?' Jock laughed at that. Silly little musical puns always amused him. 'You'll have a coffee, Major Scott, Scott, Scott.' He rushed forward. 'No, no, no, no: don't move. I'll get it for you. Aye. Sugar, is it? And a dash of angostura? D'you take cream in your coffee? Do you not? Yon's very sophisticated. Isn't it, Major Macmillan?'

'I'm sure I wouldn't know.'

Jock reproved him. 'Oh don't say that: if you don't know then there's nobody as does know and we must have one or two to keep the tone up.'

It was all an agony to Jimmy Cairns. Meantime the subalterns were trying to hide themselves in their chairs, dreading the moment when their name should be called.

'Mr Simpson?'

'Yep?'

'Yep. Is it not sophisticated to take your coffee black?'

'Not specially, I shouldn't have thought.'

'Not specially he shouldn't have thought. Which means no, I think: but he's not just sure.' He ran on with hardly a pause. 'Yon was Command at Edinburgh on the 'phone. The c.o., I says, is away out flying a kite, but I'll take a message. The mannie was very anxious. A lot of look heres, and shouldn't-have-thoughts and all that caper. D'you think he takes his coffee black?'

Jock turned. He paused, and saw them all about him.

'Oh, my babies!' he said with a sudden indulgent smile. Then sadly he repeated it, 'Oh, my babies!'

They all sat quiet.

'It seems there's got to be a contingent from Campbell Barracks at this tattoo they have for the Festival, and they're having a meeting about it. When d'you think? Was it sugar you said, Major Scott?'

'Three lumps.'

'Oh, that's not sophisticated at all.'

Jimmy tried to interrupt here. 'It's time we got on with the work,' he said, moving; but Jock kept him in his place with a flat movement of his hand.

'Tonight. All the councillors and patrons and so forth are

busy civilians you see: they can only manage tonight: they're sorry and that, so the mannie said. The mannie was a brigadier, so he said. And with the voice of a captain! Well, well, Charlie here's your coffee. Here it is. And now I'll cater for myself.'

'Has someone to go across to Edinburgh now?'

'A-huh. That's the way of it. An officer. Have we any volunteers?' Nobody moved. 'Good for you laddies: I've never liked volunteers . . . This coffee's awful unwilling. It comes in wee drips.' He looked tired again.

'Not just any officer. Field rank. And away out of here at four o'clock. Well I'd go myself but . . . well it mightn't be the best thing, if Jimmy's got to have a serious word with me, whatever that might be about. Two of you have got your wives to go home to, and Macmillan's got his Bentley motor car to keep him warm. It's an independent sort of person . . . mind you he'll probably get a good dinner.'

Charlie crashed his coffee on the table.

'All right, all right, all right. I take it this is an order.'

Jock feigned surprise. His eyebrows shot up. He dropped a teaspoon.

'That's very good of you, Major Scott.'

'Righto, let's get it straight. Four o'clock train. Will I be met?'

'In a bloody Daimler I'd say. I wouldn't be surprised if they had the red carpets down. Now, Charlie, you're sure you had no plans for this evening? I mean if there's any-thing . . .'

'Oh, for crying out loud.' Charlie looked extremely angry. Glancing at his watch, he stood up and adjusted the belt of his battledress so his kilt lay smoothly. Then he looked at Jock.

'You ought to go to bed.'

'Oh, I'm studying hard just now for this Staff College. Didn't you hear? I'm keen to be a brigadier. And with the manners of a corporal. Aye.'

'You can have my room. I'll be clear in five minutes.'

'You've plenty of time . . .'

Charlie paid no attention to him now and Jock just sat grinning and stirring his coffee. Charlie turned to the Orderly

Officer, the only one wearing tunic and Sam Browne, and a very new Sam Browne at that.

'MacKinnon. Fix a jeep would you? Ten minutes.'

'Righto, sir.'

In spite of all the rules nobody had ever got used to calling MacKinnon by his christian name.

When the others, except for Dusty Millar, who was sound asleep in the corner, had drifted away, Jimmy came across to Jock who was still stirring his cold coffee. He hesitated, and leaving the spoon in the cup, Jock looked up, and he laid a hand on Jimmy's arm.

'Dinny fash yoursel', laddie. I don't want to talk about it.'

'But, Jock, I ought to tell you the whole thing.'

'No, no. Let's leave it, laddie.' A look of real pain crossed his face and made him blink his eyes. 'There's nothing we can do. Away you go.'

A moment later, Jock laid down the coffee, undrunk, and he wandered out of the room, touching things as he went, with a sort of idleness.

He met Charlie on the upstairs landing. The wood in the corridor had newly been scrubbed and it smelt like a schoolroom at the beginning of term, part clean, part damp, part musty. Charlie was carrying a little canvas case, and he looked up at Jock. His eyes were large and resentful.

'Mm?'

'Look, laddie, I was joking really. If you've fixed to see Mary, I'll go mysel' or I'll get one of the others.'

'For Christ's sake.'

'Charlie, are you mad at me? Are you?' Jock was very serious and he was speaking quickly now.

'All's fair in love and war,' Charlie said with a crooked smile.

Jock's hands reached out. 'Man, there's no question of love. I don't care about Mary . . . It was a joke. You were mad at me.'

Charlie shrugged. 'You took such a bloody long time about it.'

'Aye, I was a bore. I was trying to be funny, mind. But

it seems I'm no so amusing any more. Not any more. Just a wee bit boring.' He gave a little smile.

'It's not important,' Charlie said.

'Aye and it is. Mary was saying that the other day: saying I was a bore.'

'Chum, you're shagged out. Go sleep. You look all in.'

'No hard feelings, Charlie?'

Charlie was just about to go downstairs and he turned.

'Old boy, you're going to need that sleep.'

Jock understood. 'It's like that, is it?'

Charlie opened his mouth, then closed it again. ''Fraid so.'

'Och, it'll be all right in the end.'

'Good boy.' And as if he were frightened to say more he ran downstairs, like a much younger man. Jock watched him go, and he was thoughtful and he was sad. Then he snapped his fingers and marched along to the bedroom, where he lay down, covering himself with rough blankets. He gave a long sigh, with a waist to it, and clasping his hands behind his head, he closed his eyes.

FOUR

Barrow went to Charlie's room obliquely. He was determined to collect himself. First, when he heard voices in the bathroom he walked as far as that door and paused, listening. Then he opened it softly, and entered, sideways. Simpson and Douglas Jackson were in there and Barrow nodded, shyly. Jackson was in the shower, proudly watching the water trickle down his white body. Simpson, looking rather pink and exhausted was sitting across the bath, watching the brown water swirl in. The room was warm with steam. Simpson jumped up and said 'Hello, sir!' with a friendly nod, which Barrow returned, then he continued to mix the water in his bath. Jackson, unaware of the Colonel's arrival was singing a marching song, loudly and flatly.

Barrow smiled uncertainly and walked a few steps into the narrow room, his shoulder brushing the wall. He was still wearing his kilt, but he had taken off his battledress top, and put on a cardigan. He was wearing bedroom slippers, and he pretended he had been asleep.

He smiled a little more firmly, as Simpson stood up and pushed back the hair on his forehead.

'You chaps been playing squash or something?'

'Wish we had, sir. 'Fraid there's no squash court in barracks.'

'No?' The Colonel looked concerned. 'I'd forgotten. None nearby?'

Simpson shook his head. 'I haven't found one.'

'Pity. You're a bit of a hand at squash, aren't you, Simpson? I seem to remember you won some cup.'

'Oh, I don't know.'

'Don't be modest. Never be too modest. If you're good at something, say so.'

Simpson looked at him curiously and Barrow halted. Jackson stopped singing and then suddenly Barrow started talking again. He had to talk loudly against the noise of the running water.

'Never any good at any ball game myself really, except golf. I used to play a round occasionally. I suppose it's a question of what you're brought up to. I never played much when I was young.'

Simpson said, 'I had two brothers. They were always playing games. Then I can't shoot for toffee.'

'Oh, that's only practice.'

'Really?'

'Of course it is. You must come out with me one of these days. We'll soon teach you to hit. You just follow round till the barrel covers the bird, then swing through. It's not very difficult, but one needs practice. I used to be all right. I find it amusing, you know.'

Simpson turned off the taps, and now that he had finished his shower, Jackson walked forward drying his muscles and puffing out his chest. He greeted Barrow solemnly, and Barrow raised his eyebrows, as if he were surprised by the meeting.

'Hullo! Just enquiring what you two have been up to.'

Jackson looked at Simpson, and answered as if he were in a witness box.

'Eric and I have been for a run, Colonel. I hope there's nothing wrong in that.'

'Hard going in the snow?'

Jackson grunted. He would never have gone had the conditions been good. Jackson was always proving himself, lifting chairs with outstretched arms, approaching women direct in hotel lounges, climbing every mountain that presented itself.

'You been out yourself, Colonel?'

'Not yet.'

'Light's failing.'

'Mm. I thought I might take a shot at a duck. Drive out you know. Fields are flooded by the river. Duck are best at this time.'

'Mm,' Jackson said, studying the few hairs on his chest

and Simpson said secretively and importantly, 'You're remembering sir? You have something on at five-thirty.' He gave a knowing nod, keeping Jackson out of the secret, and the latter turned away as if he were not interested.

'I hadn't forgotten, Simpson.'

Simpson climbed into his bath. But when he had immersed himself in the water, and twisted round to pursue the conversation, Barrow had vanished. He went as quickly as he had appeared. Simpson was a little bewildered, then he lay back and soaped his arms. Now that Jackson and he had gone a couple of runs together, discussing hard training and the need for firmer discipline in the Battalion, they were on much more friendly terms.

'He's a bit eccentric.' Jackson nodded and Simpson went on, 'But he's a damned good man, you know. Really he is.' Jackson did not seem to have the same interest in the Colonel's sudden call. He was bending and stretching his knees.

'If I were c.o.,' he said, 'I'd make the whole Mess go for a run. Think what good it would do that fat bastard Millar.'

When the knock came the second time, Jock gave an unwilling little grunt. Barrow was pale, but he walked into the room quite swiftly, closing the door quietly but firmly behind him. Jock moved a little so that the mattress squeaked, but he did not move far enough to observe his visitor. With his eyes closed, and his face against the wall he said that Charlie was in Edinburgh.

'He's away. He'll be back the morn.'

Barrow was firm and collected. But his neck seemed to have grown longer and he stretched it frequently. He clipped his words short. He said quietly, 'Yes, I gathered that. I came to see you, actually. Did I wake you?'

Jock rolled over and looked at him with a bland eye.

'A-huh.'

'I'm so sorry. It is rather important, Jock.'

Jock seemed exhausted. He hauled himself up on one elbow and nodded his head. His hair was tousled and

spiky. He reached out for a cigarette, but the packet on
the bedside table was empty. Barrow watched him and he
felt in his cardigan pockets.

'I'm afraid I haven't brought my case.'

Jock nodded towards his battledress, flung untidily over
the chair. 'There's another packet in my pouch there. My
lighter should be in there too.'

The Colonel started to burrow for them and Jock said:

'What's the time, Colonel? I thought it was five-thirty,
our date?'

'That,' he touched his moustache, 'that was the plan. I
wanted to change it. I'm sorry to have woken you.'

He gave Jock the cigarettes, and they each took one.
Barrow tried valiantly with the lighter, taking it in both
hands at last, striking it clumsily with his forefinger. But
his hands were not steady and the gadget refused to work
and Jock grew impatient.

'Here; give.'

Barrow smiled as he handed it over.

'My hands are useless.'

'A-huh.' Jock replied, still bored, and with one sharp
movement of his big thumb he turned the steel, and the
flame appeared. Barrow gave a funny little shrug but Jock
did not smile.

'I thought you were out shooting.'

'No. I . . .' He paused. 'I decided not to go till later.'

Jock adjusted his pillow, and taking a breath of his cigarette he lay back, and stared at the ceiling, prepared to
say nothing. Barrow looked at him for a moment, then he
twisted, and moved to the far corner of the room. He stood
beside the basin, and as he talked he leant back on the
window-sill behind him.

'Jock, this is quite unofficial, you understand. I don't
know how much the others have told you. I don't know
how much you've heard.' Jock ran his tongue round his
lip, and spat away a little flick of tobacco.

'Well, actually the cat's out of the bag,' Barrow went
on hurriedly. 'I like to have things out in the open, you
understand. I know all about it.'

Jock looked at him slowly.

'If you're trying to bewilder me, Colonel, you're doing fine,' he said at last, and Barrow leant forward and started to play with the tap on the basin. He turned it off and on once or twice before he composed himself.

'I'll be quite frank, Jock. I've nothing to hide. I haven't come here to bewilder you, as you say. I've come for quite another reason.'

'A-huh.'

The tap was turned on again.

'I think you know quite well what I mean when I say the cat's out of the bag. Come, Sinclair, as I say, this is quite an unofficial visit. I know very well you struck Fraser last night.'

'You've got the evidence?'

He replied quietly, 'I said I know very well.'

'Who told you?'

'More than one person.'

'McLean?' Jock sat up and looked at him suspiciously. 'Did you say you'd seen McLean?'

'I didn't say so, but I have. Jock, this isn't the point.'

'It is for me, Colonel. Who else have you seen?'

Barrow moved impatiently.

'Please. Let me say what I have to say. I like to have things in the open. I don't like deception. But this isn't easy for me.'

Jock gave a little chuckle. 'For Christ's sake. What d'you think it is for me? A bloody picnic?'

'No.' Barrow looked at him steadily. 'No, I don't think that. I think it's very serious for you. And I'm sorry. Really sorry. I mean that.' Jock still did not reply so Barrow turned the tap on again. 'I must add . . .'

Jock couldn't hear for the splash of the water in the basin.

'For Christ's sake turn that thing off. Come again. What d'you say?'

Barrow turned off the tap, pointed his fingertips together and stretched his neck.

'I must add that I haven't come here to say that I am sorry for what I have done. No. Rather am I sorry for what I have had to do.' It was a prepared speech. The mirror rehearsal was reflected in every sentence. 'I am sorry for what has had to be done.'

'Och, to hell with all that.'

'I'm sorry.'

'A-huh. All right. Good for you. I don't know what the hell you've done, anyway.'

The Colonel did not seem to hear him. He was saying the things he had prepared himself to say, like an unpopular candidate at a political meeting, reciting his manifesto to an inattentive crowd.

'In spite of the interpretation some people may like to give to my actions I can say honestly, Sinclair, I can say truthfully, that it has not been pleasant for me. On the contrary.' He began again, 'Although our relationship has not been an easy one I myself believe this to have been entirely dictated by the circumstances in which we found ourselves. Given another set of circumstances I think I can say that we could have taken a very different view of each other. Perhaps we have in common more than is supposed . . .' He paused there. He had flung out a rope, and he waited but Jock never moved, so he was forced to go on. 'It is a pity . . . But whatever the circumstances no reasonable man can be expected to enjoy the business of hurting a brother officer . . .'

'Och, for Christ's sake.'

'Believe me Sinclair, circumstances allowed me no choice.'

'Man, you're not making sense to me at all. Just what have you done?'

Barrow shrugged. 'I have done what I considered it my duty to do. That's all. I have started formal enquiries . . . Of course, it will be a matter for Brigade.'

Jock blinked. Barrow went on, as if the details bored him. They ran out one after another.

'Oh, I checked that the stories tallied, then I had Simpson in, and then,' he shrugged. 'Then I set the ball rolling. Mr Riddick's busy now collecting formal evidence with a view to court martial.'

'Mr Riddick would be pleased,' Jock said with a snort.

'He's not a friend of yours?'

'It's a surprise to me how much you've learnt so quickly, and how much you've missed.'

Barrow smiled warily. 'That's always the way in a foreign country.'

'A-huh.' Jock was alive enough, once again, to give himself time to regain some sense of tactics. 'So you're sorry.'

'Yes. Yes I am. I don't say I shouldn't have done it. Mind you, Sinclair, I'm not here to justify myself. The decisions I took were not, I believe, the wrong ones.' He paused and looked out the window. 'But when I saw you this afternoon by the fire downstairs, I suppose I knew just how sorry I was. I genuinely hope Brigade decides to dismiss the thing. I can assure you I would support any such recommendation.'

The Colonel seemed to want to say something quite different and quite plain but his words, like his feelings, were half strangled. He turned, expecting some encouragement: some reward for his gesture. He wanted more than anything in the world the relief of a handshake. 'Well,' Jock might have said, 'There it is. Just one of those things.' Or even, 'Good of you to say so.' That was part of the equation. That would have been enough. But Jock never fought to finish with a handshake. He fought to kill.

'A-huh. Well, if you're all that sorry, do I take it you're withdrawing the enquiries, eh? Do I take this as the rap over the knuckles. Is that it?'

Barrow was stiff and collected again. 'I wish you could. I'm afraid that's out of the question.'

'What d'you mean? Has the report gone off?'

'No . . . No, I haven't even seen it. The charges haven't been formulated. But it must be common news by now. Mr Riddick's started.'

'You could still refuse to pass the case up farther. Say you're dealing with it yourself . . . Well, couldn't you?'

'You know I couldn't. It's a court-martial offence.'

'You're still the Colonel.'

The Colonel swallowed: 'That's exactly what I mean.'

'Och, to hell with you, Barrow. Are you a man or a book? You said yourself, you said to Jimmy, you're only here a year or two. You'll be away up to Brigade. You said yourself you didn't care about this lark. Didn't you?'

The Colonel shrugged. He nearly laughed.

'News gets around,' he said faintly. 'How news gets round!' Then he turned away. He got nearer to the truth than was comfortable for him.

'God in heaven, nothing's ever mattered to me more. You said a minute ago that I wasn't observant. I'm surprised at you.'

'You do care?'

'Of course I care.' he said softly. 'Isn't it everybody's dream to have his Battalion?' He was hurting himself purposely, with a sort of joy.

'Then what was all that you said to Jimmy t'other night? What was all that in aid of, eh?'

Barrow now sighed, softly.

'I suppose it was the same as the shooting this afternoon. Call it a fib.'

Jock shook his head. 'You're a bloody queer one,' he said, and leant back on his pillows. Barrow smiled rather hopelessly and he agreed.

'Yes, I suppose I am.'

'Oh, for crying out loud,' Jock said scornfully. 'You're too yellow to see me this morning, then off you go and you start all these enquiries to axe me down. Then you're in a funk again so you come and say sorry, but you're still too bloody funk to go back on yourself.'

'Yes.' Barrow's face fell. He nodded slowly. 'I suppose that's one way of looking at it. It's not actually the way I see it.'

'Och. For Christ's sake. What the hell are you?'

'I'm sorry, Jock. It would do the Battalion great harm, you know, to let a thing like this ride. It is my business to think of the Battalion. I can assure you it was that which guided me. I'm most awfully sorry.'

Jock's fists grew tight with anger. He spat as he talked, and his face grew very red.

'To hell with you, Barrow Boy. You haven't heard half of it. I've given you your chance but you wouldn't bloody take it.' He made a wide sweeping gesture. 'It's your own bloody funeral. D'you think I've no friends, eh? When it comes to it, they'll matter, and they saw you at the cocktail party,

Barrow. For Christ's sake, they've come all the way with
me. What about Charlie, eh? If it comes to court d'you no
think he'll have something to say? Aye, and what about my
Adjutant? What about Jimmy? Eh? What's he going to
say? He was a boy, Jimmy was. I taught him to be a soldier, d'you follow? D'you think he's going to say anything
except what a bloody piece of cheek it is you taking it as far
as a court?'

Barrow looked at him sadly, and let him run on. Jock
shook his head like a turkey.

'Bachch . . . it's you that'll be looking silly, I'm telling
you.'

Barrow put his hands in his cardigan pockets.

'I blame myself most for not having come and spoken to
you earlier on. We could have avoided all this.'

'Ach,' Jock said, and he leant back on his pillows again
and closed his eyes. He pretended Barrow wasn't there. But
Barrow, almost to spite himself or purge himself, seemed
determined to go on. He went on and on, although Jock
never spoke: not a muscle of his face moved. Barrow might
have been talking to a stone and he knew this very well.
Indeed he spoke as if he were addressing trees. He spoke
at length, but apparently without feeling. His voice was as
resigned as a ghost's. The pitch of it never rose or fell. And
Jock never replied. They might have been ignorant of each
other's presence.

'. . . That's why, I suppose, it meant so much to me. As a
matter of fact I've always wanted to be with the Battalion, and
somehow I've always been moved on elsewhere. But I know a
great deal about it, you know. Perhaps you'd be surprised to
hear I'm writing a history of it now. That's why I've such an
admiration for you. I have. I . . . I know that desert campaign
as if I'd been there myself. The night you took over, in the
light of the flares. Five hundred were killed and wounded
that night. Five hundred and forty-two officers and men,
to be precise. Quite a battle. The wounded put their rifles,
bayonet in the ground, to mark where they were. And you
brought in the carriers, wasn't that it? Somebody had a
phrase for you—I think it was the Pipe-Major—"Like
a Bobby at a tattoo," he said.'

His words fell on the air. The only other noise was the faint scraping of the shovels as the detention squad continued to scrape clear the square outside.

'I was in gaol, as you put it: I was cooped up then with some very unpleasant Japs. But I said I'd get back to the Battalion: back to Scotland. I loved it here, you know, as a subaltern. Even the weather had a sort of thrill for me. I used to look out at this barrack square and dream that one day I . . . I knew a lot of people who have gone away.'

'For Christ's sake.' Jock still kept his eyes closed.

'Of all people, I'm sorry I should have had to do this to you. Then perhaps that's fate. D'you ever feel that you're just playing out some move that's already been arranged for you? D'you feel that?'

'Never.'

'Oh. That's how I've felt. I . . .'

'Look, I'm tired. I'm played out.'

'Yes, I'm sorry. You look tired. Well at least I've said something of what I'd meant to say. I can't expect you to forgive me now, but I do hope, in the future, sometime, you'll . . .' His voice trailed away, and there was a pause.

Then suddenly Barrow sounded angry; angry with Jock for his rudeness, but more angry with himself. He began to sweat a little.

'No man is bigger than the Battalion, Jock. That's what I've had to remember. So don't misinterpret me. I didn't come here to apologize for my actions. Oh no. I came here to say I was sorry that it had to be you. Sorry you'd made such a damned ass of yourself. There it is then; there it is.'

Jock lay absolutely still, waiting for him to leave. Then at last, very suddenly, Barrow said, 'Of course you're tired,' and with that same little stretch of his neck, he left the room, as if he'd just called to borrow a cigarette.

'Yes? What is it, Sergeant-Major?'

Mr Riddick never enjoyed being called Sergeant-Major but this was a mistake Barrow often made when he was in an impatient mood.

Mr Riddick had caught him just outside the Battalion H.Q. offices. He had a board with several important papers attached to it tucked smartly underneath his arm, as if it were a drill stick.

Barrow looked hopelessly round the square as he waited for Mr Riddick to speak. He looked at the barracks as if it were a prison from which there was no escape. The sky itself was like a low roof.

Mr Riddick took some time to compose himself. Barrow pitched his weight back on one heel and knocked a little bit of hard snow to the side of the path with the toe of his other foot.

'Well, what is it?'

'Sir. Been talking with the Pipe-Major, sir. I believe he's had a word with the Adjutant.'

Barrow stared into his face, half savage and half bored.

'Go on, go on.'

When he was uncertain of himself Mr Riddick talked louder than ever.

'Perhaps we're being a little hasty with this enquiry, sir.'

'What did you say?'

'Sir. Wouldn't express an opinion of this sort unless I felt it was the over-all opinion of the non-commissioned ranks, sir. It does seem as how they feel such an enquiry would do more harm . . .'

'Mr Riddick, you astonish me.'

'Sir.'

'I thought I gave an order that the evidence should be collected.'

'Sir. I understood the order, sir.'

'Well, dammit, obey me.'

'Sir.'

Barrow relaxed a little.

'Of course, this can't be a popular order. But it is an order. It's the good of the Battalion we must think of.'

'Begging your pardon, sir, it was the good of the Battalion we were considering. Feel the Battalion might be best served if you were to deal with this little matter yourself, sir. Battalion would support you, sir.'

'There's no question of that, d'you hear me?' Barrow could have been heard a hunded yards off. 'No question of it. Dammit, the Sergeants' Mess isn't a senate.'

'Sir.'

Barrow lowered his voice.

'For God's sake, Mr Riddick, if an officer strikes an other rank he has to pay for it, hasn't he? Well, hasn't he?'

'Sir.'

'Well, get cracking with it.'

'Sir. Considered it my duty to raise it, sir.'

'Very well. You raised it. Now get on with it.'

'Sir.'

A tremendous salute followed and the R.S.M. about-turned and marched off. Barrow watched him, and he fidgeted. Mr Riddick would not have raised the question unless the pressure had been very strong: he loathed Jock.

This would be a perfect opportunity to redress some of the damage. As he thought of that, Barrow heard his own light voice echo in his ears. The banalities were like a chorus. The good of the Battalion. Duty. Honesty. There was something false about the very sound of the name Sinclair, as it fell from his lips.

'Mr Riddick?'

Had Mr Riddick come back to him it might have been different but he did not. He halted some twenty paces away and he shouted from there. His voice echoed giddily round and round the cold square.

'Sir!'

'Mr Riddick, I . . .' Barrow's hands fell limp. He twitched his moustache. 'I want that report tonight,' he said flatly. The echo of his voice was tired and high and it was smothered by Mr Riddick's final '*Sir!*'

Still Barrow did not move. Then at last a little orderly from the office came out of the block and approached him. The Orderly gave an affected salute. His battledress was creased smartly in every direction and his bonnet had been clipped and shaped. The Orderly spent his evenings reshaping the clothes with which he was issued. Barrow stared at him with undisguised hatred.

'Please, sir, d'you wish a doughnut with your tea, sir?'

Barrow screwed up his face.

'A *what?*'

'Sir, some of the lads have doughnuts with their tea on

Mondays, Wednesdays and Fridays. We get them across at the Naafi. They're fourpence each, sir, but they're very good. I strongly recommend them, I do.' The Orderly smiled his mother's smile. 'I could arrange it, sir.'

'Not for me.'

'Colonel Sinclair always used to like one.'

'I don't care what Colonel Sinclair liked for his tea.'

The reproof did not seem to upset the Orderly. 'No, sir; I thought I'd just ask you.'

'O God,' Barrow said suddenly, 'O God.'

That afternoon at five o'clock the flag had been lowered and Retreat had been played. But sundown was a technical point. The sun had been hidden behind a bank of cloud all day. Corporal Fraser took the pipes and drums back to the Band Block and it was his last duty of the day to see that the piping room was cleaned up and tidy.

'Corporal, there's a friend of yours out there, his bottom out behind him,' Piper Adam said.

Fraser was waiting patiently for all the kit to be cleaned and cleared away. He turned round slowly, and he looked down to the square to see Jock marching slowly across. It was just light enough for him to be recognizable, a black figure against the snow.

'Is he no a friend of yours, Corporal, eh? Is he no a friend any longer?'

'D'you see that broom over there, Adam?'

'No, Corporal. I don't see it.'

'Get over to it and start away.'

'It's no my turn for the sweeping.'

One of the other pipers, a serious boy with steel-rimmed glasses, now said, 'What's that he's marching at, Corporal?'

The Corporal turned back again. He said slowly.

'Jock always marches at 120 to the minute.'

'It's no as fast as that. Not nearly as fast as that,' Adam said. 'Maybe it's the weight on his mind that slows him down.'

'You talk too much.'

'That's a terrible black eye you've got, Corporal. It looks terrible sore.'

'Get on.'

'Corporal, I'm sympathizing with you. That's what I'm doing.'

The other piper said wistfully, 'Whatever it is he never

changes his pace. Look at his footsteps, too. If the steps were there in front of him he'd put his foot right in them.'

'It's no where he put his feet that worries the Corporal. It's where he puts his fist.'

'Your mouth's too big, Piper Adam.'

'That's a personal remark, Corporal.'

'If you don't get on you'll no get out the night.'

'I've no money to go out the night.'

'Then you'll go on a charge.'

'That's bloody victimization, Corporal. That's what that is.'

'You'll be telling that to the Pipe-Major, d'you hear me?'

'Och.'

'D'ye hear me?'

Piper Adam at last obeyed but as he moved across the room he continued to mumble.

'. . . and it's the bloody fiddle I should a' taken up. No these pipes at all. I'm telling yous. There's no all this bull in the Hallé. Aye, I'm telling you.'

The Corporal turned to the square, but it was empty now. Jock was on his way. It was as bare as oblivion.

Jock went down the dark alley to the stage-door, and without a word of explanation he passed a ten-shilling note to the porter behind the window. The porter winked and welcomed him back, but Jock only nodded. He threw the note to the man as if he were throwing it overboard, and then he walked up the stone steps. Turning to his left he climbed the narrow staircase to the second floor where Mary had her dressing-room. She was not there, but the unshaded overhead light had been left on, and the room had hardly changed since he had known it. Over the light-switch was a notice scrawled in lipstick on the lid of a shoe-box: *Please turn me off*. It was balanced on the top of the switch. The walls were badly in need of redecoration; the dressing-table, which had been bought at some sale years before, was as untidy as ever, and the big mirror still had a postcard slipped into the corner and one or two official notes pinned on to the frame. All around the room budding actors and actresses had scrawled their names on the walls, but none of the names meant anything now. The sash of the window was broken and Jock walked across to try and force the top shut, but he had struggled with it before, in vain. At the top right-hand corner there was a gap of two or three inches. The window seemed to be set in a wall which was only one brick deep. Jock felt that if he shoved with his shoulder then the side of the room might collapse with a rumble into the alley below. He grasped hold of the shutters and pulled them together. The bar to lock them had broken off its coupling and the draught through the window pushed them open again. But the room was cold. Methodically he carried a chair across and placed it against the shutters to hold them close. There was a gas fire burning low in one corner and he turned it up.

Finding the kettle half filled he lit the gas ring too, and put the kettle on. He had to kneel down to adjust it. Then with his knuckles he pushed his weight back and he squatted in front of the fire, warming his hands. At last he stepped back and sat on a little chair with a plywood seat which creaked as it took his weight. The legs were loose and he rocked gently, in a little circle, holding on to the seat at his sides. He was sick with tiredness now, and the gas fire made him nod. His eyes were smarting, and he was too exhausted to find himself a cigarette. He did not get up when he heard her coming: his chair creaked as the door opened and she entered, but he still could not be bothered to climb to his feet. He looked over his shoulder and said just, 'Mary.'

'Laddie, they never told me you were here.'

'I thought I'd find you. I know my way. I mind it fine.'

She moved with a rustle. She was wearing a long grey dress that did not bear close inspection. It had been mended and remended and the hem was very dirty. The lace at the sleeve was pink-brown with grease paint and the apron was marked with dust. They were performing an adaptation of *The Heart of Midlothian*, and Jeanie Deans was one of Mary's star parts. Almost like a professional, because Jock never thought of her as a professional, she took some cotton wool and began to clean some of the make-up from round her eyes.

'I'll get the sack if they find you here. How did you get in?'

'I tipped Mac.'

'Och,' she said. 'There was no need to have done that. What did you give him?'

'Ten bob.'

'Ten bob!' She was astonished. 'Laddie, that's far too much.'

He shrugged, and climbed wearily to his feet. She was watching him in the mirror and now she turned. That smile of hers was not there any longer.

'Ten bob's about as much as I make for each performance.'

'I didn't think.' All the time he stared at her, with a sadness, and because she found his stare unnerving she turned away. But she was courteous, and she was kind. She was even tender.

'Let me help you with your coat. You'll just catch a cold when you get out again. Did you close the shutters?'

'A-huh.'

'That's nice of you.' She took the coat from him and she hung it on one of the pegs which was already laden with clothes and hangers.

'Untidy as ever,' Jock said and he attempted a smile.

'In this room it's not worth being anything else; well, is it?' She went on; 'Now why did you tip Mac like that? You're a terrible man.'

'I thought maybe Charlie was here before me. I thought then that Mac would need some persuading.'

'Charlie's in Edinburgh.'

'I know. I sent him. He was sore about that.'

'You're right there.'

'Did he have a date with you? I told him if he had, I'd get someone else. It was a joke. It was a joke that went wrong.'

'It'll do him no harm,' she said, 'no harm at all. Charlie's a cool one.' She brought her lips tightly together when she had said that. Then she looked at him again. She looked hard at his face, and about his eyes. She said with a sudden surge of pity:

'I'm glad you came, Jock. I'm glad. Laddie, you're worn out. I can see it in your face.'

'I've got reason to be.'

The kettle was beginning to boil and she knelt down to attend to it. She was reaching for the teapot, not looking at

Jock at all when she said, 'I know you have. I know fine, Jock. Charlie was here.'

'Ach, well.'

'But he wasn't here long after he'd told me, Jock,' she said suddenly, looking up at him. 'I got it all out of him, and I'm glad you sent him off. You were right to. When he told me it all, I sent him away myself, and if you'd not come here I was going to try and find you. It's a shame, Jock.'

'It's just a fact.' His palms turned outwards. 'That's all it is. It must have been written down somewhere. I never thought at all. I might have been one of your actors. I just played out the lines, and I struck the laddie and ever since then, Mary, I've been following my own footsteps. They lead me hither and thither.'

'Is it real serious?'

He touched the dust on the narrow mantelpiece. 'Sometimes I tell myself it isn't. There's lots of ifs and buts to it. But just as I see the way out, just as I see the light and I see the chance, I know fine at the same time just how bloody serious it is. Maybe the same devils as saved me before have turned the thing against me now.'

'Och, away you go. The devil takes care of his ain.'

'Oh, dearie me,' he said suddenly and with a sigh he sat down on the little chair again so she was by his feet where she sat. She had found cups and she poured out the tea. Then she said,

'I told Charlie I'd never see him again.'

'You what?'

'You heard. He'd no right to do that.'

'It's none of Charlie's fault.'

'Barrow would have never dared to move without him.'

'But Barrow has moved. I've just seen him. He came to say he's sorry.' He laughed. 'That was comic.'

Then he waved his hand in the air wiping out all they had said.

'Och, Charlie didn't come into it lassie.'

She handed him up the cup. 'Did they not tell you, then? Did you not hear what happened?'

Jock looked at her suspiciously. He felt a little frightened of what she was about to say. She must have had a right row with Charlie. But he had not come to discuss all this. He had come to see her and to forget it. She looked at him cautiously as he replied very slowly:

'I know fine what happened. Barrow's just told me. It was the doctor who gave the show away, then Mr McLean had to see him too. It had nothing to do with Charlie.'

She shook her head. 'Are you blind, Jock? I saw it coming last night; for heaven's sake. He didn't like it when you called. Did you not see that?'

Jock blinked. He had long been trained in the school which teaches that women are the trouble-makers, and it was not the first time that he and Charlie had had the same girl. But it had never destroyed their friendship, and it never would.

'You're away off net.'

'That I'm not. D'you fancy I'd just say a thing like that?'

'No.'

'Charlie told me, Jock. He told me himself. Barrow had him in. He asked him what he thought. He asked him if he ought to chase the rumour up.'

Jock sat very stiffly, with his knees together, and he looked down at her, awkwardly, with his chin in his collar.

'You've had words with Charlie.'

'When he said that I had words with him, I . . .'

'Before that you'd had a tussle with him.'

'No.'

He looked at her solemnly. 'You're no in love with him any more?'

'With Charlie?' She shook her head and gave a weak little laugh. 'Of course I'm not in love with him. For heaven's sake, I never have been.'

'You were carrying on with him,' he said hotly, and she put a hand on his knee.

'Och, Jock Sinclair. You're a child. You're a child.'

He looked angry now; hurt that she should make a fool of him. He moved a little in his chair and he looked away from her as he said,

'Did Charlie say he'd seen Barrow?'

'Yes.'

'He never told me.'

'Maybe he wasn't going to.'

He flared up at that. He rose to his feet and his cup rattled in the saucer.

'That's an awful thing to say. Charlie'd tell me. Charlie's no a sneak. It's just that he hasn't had time. Did he tell you what he said to Barrow? Did he?'

She shrugged. 'The enquiry's gone forward, hasn't it?'

Jock looked back at her, over his shoulder.

'Charlie'd never have done that out of spite, if he did it at all.' He seemed to be angry with her, not anybody else. When he started his voice was low, but it grew louder all the time. 'Women like you don't understand. You see us when we're drunk and playing the fool. You never know the real men. You don't see the other side. Aye, maybe Charlie was called in.' He walked as far as the wall at the other side of the room and he pushed his fist against it, softly, once or twice. She sat very still, with her cup in her lap. Everything looked bare and yellow in that light.

'Aye, and maybe when he was told the facts he saw his duty. He's a good officer, Charlie. When it comes to it he knows what's right and what's wrong. If you sent him away with a flea in his ear, you did wrong. If he had to do that to me, then he had to do that to me, and maybe he was right to. But he'd never want to. Not Charlie.'

She watched him solemnly, and his eyes were brimming and burning with a sort of hot pride. Then she looked down at her cup, and she moved it to her side.

'You know I've never tried to make trouble.'

'I know nothing about you. Nothing at all.'

She was hurt, and he saw that he had hurt her. His own face screwed up with the same pain that he had inflicted. She had turned her face to the wall.

'Mary, I'm sorry, I shouldn't have said that. I'm sorry I said it. Really I am.'

She still kept her head turned away, and he moved forward clumsily. He did not know what to do so he bent down, and with the flat of his palm he stroked the top of her hair, stiffly but softly, as he would stroke the head of a dog.

'It's no business of mine,' she said at last, her voice a pitch higher, but she was not crying.

'Aye, it is. I came along to you. I'm sorry, Mary, I'm

clack-handed. I didn't mean to be angry with you. I know
you did me fine, and I'm glad of that. But you're wrong
about Charlie. He wouldn't do what you think he's done.
Och, lassie, in a battalion, it's difficult you see: whoever
it is, whatever the circumstances—Christ, you can't have
officers bashing corporals. That's just the way of it. I know
that fine. I'd have said the same thing myself. I'd have done
the same.'

She looked up at him and she just said, 'Never in a hundred years, Jock.' He opened his eyes wide: he hesitated,
and he nearly lost his way. Then he turned round, and the
fist banged back into the palm of the hand again and again.
She went on talking in a low voice, but with such conviction.

'Never in a hundred years. And you know that, fine, don't
you? Oh, Jock, you're always talking about your soldiers,
and your Battalion, but it's you that doesn't see the half of
your men. And for all your mucking and binding, and all
your nonsense, laddie, you're . . . you're a child, Jock.'

'Och, for Christ's sake,' he said. She had often said this
to him and it always irritated him.

'You expect too much of them. You expect them all to
be the same as yourself, and you're twice the man of any
of them. I mean that. You're too good for them. I've never
said it before because your head would grow too big. But it's
true. It's true.'

He said sadly. 'No, lassie. It *was* true. It *was* true. But it
isn't true any more.'

'Well, tell me a better man, eh? Is Macmillan better?
Who are all the others? What about Barrow?'

He shook his head and he dropped his weight on to the
chair again.

'Och, to hell with all that,' he said. 'I'm about awa' with it
now. I don't know which'll bust first, my head or my heart.
So to hell with all that. C'mon out with me.'

She looked up at the round clock face above the door.
'Laddie, I can't. I've another show in half an hour.'

'What is it tonight?'

'Jeanie Deans.'

'Aye,' he said and slowly he smiled. 'I saw the bill. That's
what it is. And Mary Titterington in the big letters.'

'Don't bully me. Don't bully me now.'

'No.' He put his head on one side. 'But it must give you a wee thrill. Just a wee one.'

She closed her eyes for a second.

'Let's not have all this again, Jock.'

'But I'm not mocking.'

'Oh, for heaven's sake.' She rose to her feet. 'Look I'll tell you. You see that wall. Twelve years ago, Jock, twelve years ago, before you ever had your war I was here, in this dressing-room. I was playing Effie Deans then, and I was good, though I say it myself. And I wrote my name up there with the rest of them. Oh, for heaven's sake.'

'Did you? Maybe I saw you then. Where's your name? Where is it?'

She turned away. 'When I came back I rubbed it out.'

'Och.' He looked genuinely sad. He gave a kind smile. 'Och, you shouldn't have done that. Lassie, when I was your age I was a Corporal-Piper; you've plenty time. C'mon, we'll make you write it again. C'mon.' He touched her tenderly.'

'Not for anything.'

'Och, well,' he said with a little kick of his head. 'I'll sign it for you. And shall I put mine by it?' He got out a pencil. 'Eh? Maybe I'll play Hamlet yet. Hamlet it is; is it not? That's for me, eh?'

'No,' she tried to stop him but he was determined and he reached high above her. She took it all seriously.

'What'll I put, eh?'

'I'll never talk to you again,' she said angrily as he paid no attention to her.

'What about this, eh?' He wrote down something and then he stood back with a great grin. Pretending to be very angry she looked gloweringly at what was written. '*Rex Harrison and Mary Titterington.*'

'Is that not good eh?' He said, 'Sexy Rexy: does that not fit the bill? Is that not me, eh?' He waited.

She clenched her fists, and she was shaking.

'Oh, Jock,' she said and she was suddenly in tears. 'Christ alive, you're a lovely man.' She shouted out loud, 'Oh, Jock. Jock, man, you're a bloody king.'

'Mary, Mary.' He opened his arms and comforted her. 'Come away with you. You mustn't cry.' He spoke tenderly and he held her close to him. 'You'll have me greeting too, and that'll never do. That'll never do, lassie.'

'It's not Charlie that I love,' she said hopelessly. 'Not Charlie at all.'

'But you turned me away.'

'I never, I never. I'd never turn you away. You're too good for them all.'

Suddenly it all seemed to frighten Jock. She was hugging closely to him and he pushed her back gently, to look at her, but she kept her face downcast.

'I'm a mess,' she said. 'Don't look at me, Jock. I don't want you to look at me now.'

He held her stiffly, and with hard lips he kissed her brow, by the border of her hair. He asked innocently, 'Are you saying that you love me, Mary?'

It was agony for her. 'Jock, of course I am. Of course I am. Like any other woman that's ever known you,' she said and she looked up at him for a second. 'And I'm no sure it isn't every man, too.'

He laughed at that. He tried to make it all a joke. 'Here, here, now. That's a very sophisticated sort of notion. That's too complex for me.'

'I used to be a very sophisticated girl.' She dried her eyes. 'In London.'

'And Edinburgh. And here. Until I knew you.'

'Did I drag you down?'

'You could drag me anywhere. I'd burn at the stake—so there; that's love for you.' Jock let her burrow her head in his shoulder, pushing at him so his weight fell back on his heels. She clasped him tightly.

'I love you, Jock; I love you: I've said it.'

'No, no,' he said upset, but still holding her. 'No you mustn't say that, lassie.'

'But I do.'

'You don't really. You're just upset.'

'I do, I do.' Her hands were clasped tightly on his arms.

He soothed her again, with hands and arms, looking anxiously over her shoulder.

'I tell you what, Mary. We'll have supper tonight, eh? Morag's left me now. Morag's gone away. So we'll have supper just for old times' sake. I'll pick you up here and we'll go across to the Welcome. That's what we'll do. I'll choose a good menu, and we'll have a wine too, the whole thing. Just you and me, late on.'

'Not just for old times' sake.'

He nodded, 'No, not just for old times' sake.'

'Jock, whatever they do to you . . .' but he wouldn't let her go on. He patted her back.

'I know, I know. I know you'd be good to me . . . Will you have supper, eh?'

'Mm.'

'And the wine?'

She nodded vigorously, swallowing to control herself again.

'Mm.'

'Smoked salmon and the whole lot, eh?'

'And coffee.'

'Aye, and Drambuie too.'

She said, 'Then will you come back?'

He looked at her solemnly and cautiously as she dabbed her eyes.

'Mary, I've done you enough harm as it is. I've done enough damage. I'm down on my luck, but there's no need for you . . .' He couldn't go on. He just shook his head.

'I want you to come home with me.' Her face hid nothing now. She stared at him with a sort of blank passion.

'Oh, lassie, you're kind . . .' he said and he took hold of her again and hugged her tight. He closed his eyes for a moment. 'Aye well, to hell with them all,' he said with a great sigh, and he whispered to her, 'and all their bloody enquiries, we'll forget all them. We'll make love, like the old times. Maybe again and again, after our supper. We'll make love, lassie, we'll make love.'

But even as he spoke, and patted her, his mind wandered away. She seemed to sense this and she pushed closer and closer to him in despair while he looked over her shoulder into the long mirror at the sad soldier there.

SIX

When he reached the hotel he nearly turned back again.
There was a giggling girl wheeling the revolving door, and
her partner was chasing after her, rocking forward on his
toes as he walked, with the sort of totter that irritated Jock.
The girl was in a long tulle dress of grey and pink, and she
had a travelling rug wrapped round her. That was the joke:
she'd forgotten her coat, or thrown it out of the car window.
When she arrived in the hall people turned to her. She said
she was so poor she had to use Johnny's car rug to cover her
now. She thought she was rather fetching as a peasant.

'Excuse me,' Jock said. 'If I can get past.'

They were holding some sort of dance and the hall and
lounges were crowded with people talking at a high pitch.
The older men looked well polished, the younger men looked
arrogant, and the middle men seemed to be searching for
their parties. There was a sound of a band coming from the
ballroom at the back, and people were preparing to waltz.
The ladies were dragged away to the dance floor, still looking
back and talking, while they searched for somewhere to leave
their handbags. All the available sills and shelves were already
covered with handbags of sequins and brocade.

Amongst the white shirts and the black coats, squeez-
ing between the bare shoulders of the women, Jock felt
self-conscious in his khaki and he did not enjoy the sen-
sation. Two or three people he knew nodded as he went
through, and others a little farther away talked in urgent
whispers: 'My *dear*, look. There's Jock Sinclair. What *do*
you suppose?'

'A-huh,' Jock said, and 'A-huh,' as he passed.

He got as far as the cocktail bar, but it was full of dancers.
Macmillan was there, draped against the bar, talking to a
lady torpedo with eyes like a fish. The dress she had chosen

was salmon-pink, but she flushed a deeper colour than that when she recognized Jock.

'Sandy, *tell* me. How absolutely *awful*. D'you suppose he heard? D'you suppose?' She straightened. 'My dear boy, I don't care a rap if he did. Not I. But do tell me.'

Sandy shook his head and took a sip of his drink. He nodded politely to Jock.

'Not dancing?'

Jock shouted across two heads and a torpedo's back.

'Not me. What's the caper?'

'Spinsters of the district. Spinsters' ball.'

Jock did not find a reply. He turned away, and the effect was of rudeness.

'What was I saying?' the torpedo said, pleased that her description of Jock's manners should have been demonstrated so accurately. 'Sandy, what did I say? What did I? No manners at all!'

'Yes, quite,' Sandy said, nodding, glancing sideways in search of relief.

'Of course. But of course. *Just* what I was saying. Now Barrow Boy's *very* different, but well, I always say if a man . . .'

'He was sorry he couldn't come tonight.'

'Nonsense. He refuses everything.'

'He's awfully busy.'

'Pooh, to that! My dear, let me tell you that before the war officers at the Mess—officers and gentlemen, isn't that what they say?'

'That's right.'

'Sandy, of course, you're a gentleman. You're always the same. Now what was I saying?'

'I beg your pardon?'

'Sandy, I do believe you're not attending to me.'

'Isn't the band noisy?'

'Yes. Look at that awful man now.'

'Who's this?'

'That Sinclair, leaning over whispering to the barman like that. What a big sit-upon he has, Sandy. Not a well-bred sit-upon at all, no. I suppose the barman's his best friend. I suppose that's it.'

When she looked round, Sandy had turned away.

'Carol,' he was saying. 'How glorious to see you.'

The torpedo just pounced on the nearest person. 'I do think that Sinclair man is frightful, don't you?'

'Too awful.' So the music went around and around.

Jock went upstairs to find the manager, but he was to be disappointed. The head waiter was the only person he could find, and he quickly confirmed that there was no possibility of supper after ten-thirty. It would have to be a very special arrangement in the ordinary way, but with the dance on, it was out of the question.

'Ah well,' Jock said, apparently resigned and the head waiter was all napkin and coat-tails as he bowed good-evening. As he turned away Jock heard his name called, and there beside him was the red-haired Rattray, dressed in a kilt and tweed jacket.

'Jock, it's fine to see you,' he said and he had had one or two. Rattray only needed one or two to set him off. Jock screwed up his eyes and nodded.

'A-huh,' he mumbled.

'I'm bloody chocka with all this carry-on down the stairs. Have you ever seen the likes? I saw Simpson there, and some o' the others. What are you up to, Jock? Eh, man?'

Jock seemed to be far away.

'Just a minute,' he said, and he went back to the head waiter. Rattray saw him take out a pound and offer it to him but the head waiter shook his head and refused it. He looked like a professional football player: he had blue, outdoor eyes. He smiled and said 'no' again while Jock talked harder and harder. It might have been a matter of life and death, but the waiter shook his head. Jock was disappointed. Looking rather dazed by his failure he wandered back to the top of the staircase, where Rattray awaited him.

Rattray started asking questions, and when Jock didn't answer, he just asked them again. Jock shook his head.

'Och, it was just about supper.'

'Have you not had your supper? Man, you didn't have lunch, I saw that. You need food. You looked washed out. Aye, you do.'

When they came to the bottom of the stairs something

else caught Rattray's attention and he said, 'Oh for pity's sake look at the way that puppy's wearing the kilt. It's a bloody crime.'

They had to pass this boy as they walked to the door and Jock wandered round him without difficulty, but Rattray pretended he could not get past. He braced his shoulders and he said, 'If you'll excuse me.'

The young man looked round surprised.

'I said if you'll excuse me.'

'I'm so sorry.' He stepped to one side, and Rattray flicked his head like a Nazi, and marched squarely to the door. Jock was already outside and had nearly escaped him, but Rattray was soon at his side. When he was in this mood he talked right into people's faces and now he suggested a plan of campaign to Jock. They would get a sandwich at the Palace Bar, where men were men. Jock looked wearily at the freckled face, green in the street light, the crinkly hair and the uneven teeth, and eventually he allowed himself to be taken along. He was only vaguely conscious of Rattray's hand on his elbow and he hardly listened to his talk at all. This was probably a good thing, as Rattray was the world's worst comforter. He kept saying how he would never have ruined Jock in the way the others were doing. He said what he would do if he were Brigade.

'But we've got to face the facts. Brigade's not like that. And Brigade's no friend of yours, I'm sure: and more's the credit to you, Jock. But we've got to face the facts.'

Jock nodded and Rattray said, 'Believe me, Jock lad, if Barrow'd called me in and not Charlie and Jimmy I'd have given him a funny answer.'

For the first time since they had met, Jock was interested. He stopped and he said quietly,

'Who did you say Barrow saw?'

'Christ, did you not know?'

'Who?'

'Jock, I thought you knew, man.' Rattray looked alarmed. 'I'm no the lad to tell tales. I thought it was common knowledge.'

'Who did you say?'

'You'll no tell them I told you, Jock?'

'I'm not interested in telling anybody anything.'

'Charlie Scott.'

'Aye, I heard that.'

'And Jimmy Cairns.'

'Not Jimmy. You made that up. You made that up, eh?'

'Jock lad, I swear. . . .'

'You can't be right.'

'Jock, I'm right enough.'

'For Christ's sake. Oh, for Christ's sake,' Jock said, then very suddenly he walked on. Tears were running down his cheeks. But as they walked and as Rattray went on, he recovered. Rattray did not see his tears.

'Aye, Jimmy too. The both of them. They were in together. Douglas Jackson got it out of Simpson who was outside the door and I got it from him.'

Jock said no more, but he looked and felt very cold and weary now, and he wondered if he was maybe going to collapse.

He said once or twice that he ought to go to the theatre to leave a message but Rattray said they could do that later. Now Rattray was explaining what was wrong with the Regiment.

'It's recruited from all over. That's what's the matter with it. I say we ought to stick to the old way. D'you know that? Look, Jock,' the face loomed in front of Jock again, pink-eyed and fanatic. 'The Regiment was based on the clan system, and Scotsmen have always fought in clans. If we got back to that, then you wouldn't be in the muck you are now. But you mustn't worry, Jock. We'll find a way. Here's the Palace now.'

'I don't want to go in.'

'You'd be better for something to eat.'

'I don't want anything to eat.'

'Och, you will. We'll have a wee dram first. C'mon, Jock, it'll pull you together.'

'You go in. I'm going on.'

Rattray braced his shoulders. 'Alec Rattray's no the lad to desert a comrade. No, no. I'll come in with you.'

'I'll manage on my own.'

'I said I'll come with you, Jock. Did you hear, man? I

can see you're in a state, and Alec Rattray's not the lad to
leave you. D'you follow?'

Jock followed, and further, Jock followed his own footsteps. He persuaded himself that he was walking home
although he knew the house would be dark and cold. He
would rest a while, recover, and return to the theatre. And
he could get rid of this Rattray. It was a strange night now,
half frosty and half damp. There was fog on the river and
it crept through the streets. The cold was penetrating and
depressing at the same time. When they had walked as far
as the same hotel that Jock had visited an age before, just
twenty-four hours before, he stopped on the threshold, and
looked into the lighted hall.

'Aye, here's a place,' Rattray said. 'C'mon in,' and he led
the way through the same little private bar, where the same
people were sitting, except for Morag and the Corporal.
There was no sign of them.

Conversation died on the lips when Jock appeared, but he
seemed quite resigned to that. He made no qualifying gesture. He unbuttoned his coat, like a man shown into a sick-
room, slowly, as if the buttons hurt the tips of his fingers.
He looked sadly round while Rattray gave a hearty welcome,
mentioning a couple of the sergeants by name.

'We'll have two big drams,' Rattray said, poking his head
under the glass, where the landlord was crouching, like an
anxious ferret.

'No, we won't,' Jock said quietly and flatly. 'I'll just have
a round of ham.'

The landlord seemed satisfied by that. He looked relieved
and he disappeared, repeating the order again and again to
himself, as if it were a word of comfort. 'And a round of
ham; aye, and a round of ham.'

The others resumed their conversations with the same
air of studied normality that the Mess had assumed that
morning, and Jock hung up his heavy coat. When he looked
at them, each one looked away, but in spite of that they did
not seemed unfriendly. Jock smiled when he recognized that
there was pity in their eyes, then he moved through the tables,
slowly, touching chairs and tables as he went, in a shy and
longing sort of way. His hands seemed to linger where they

touched: even his eyelids seemed to pause when he blinked and turned his eyes from one group to another. He found a place in a corner and there he watched one of the sergeants who had sat down on the piano-stool and opened the piano lid. But for a while the Sergeant did not begin to play. He stared at the keys as the room grew quiet, and Rattray said, 'Give us a tune.'

Rattray carried the sandwich across and Jock took a bite of it, then he looked at it as if it were made of paper. He put it back on the plate and put the plate on the glass top of the table. He began to chew, and people started to talk again.

The Sergeant at the piano let his fingers run down the scale.

Gently he played *Kelvin Grove*, and then another ballad. Soon they were calling out the names of tunes, and he was playing them. Then a drink or two later, they began to sing. Jock himself did not take a drink all evening and he did not sing, but he began to look quite happy as they went through some of the favourites. To Rattray's chagrin—'That's a Sassenach tune, for Christ's sake'—the Sergeant played some English tunes too, but they did not sing to those, so he soon returned to the Scottish ones. Like all drunk men, they got round to the sad tunes, and they sang all the Jacobite songs with sweating vigour: *The Skye Boat Song, Will ye no come back again?, Charlie is my darling, my darling*. They returned for a second time to *We're no awa' to bide awa'* and *I belong to Glasgow*.

'Aye well,' Jock said, when at last there was a pause. 'I'll be on my way.'

'There's plenty time yet.' Rattray was aflame with patriotism now. 'You can't go yet, Jock.'

'I'm tired now.'

'Och, come off it. We'll no let you go.'

For the first time Jock raised his voice.

'I said I was finished,' he said, and they shuffled away to let him through.

The pianist began again and they turned back to him, and forgot about Jock. But the proprietor was standing in the hall, hanging his head, and Jock stopped beside him.

'Was there any damage last night?'

'Och, no, Colonel Sinclair.'

'I'll pay if there was any damage.'

'I wouldn't think of it, Colonel. Let's just forget the whole incident.'

'Aye,' Jock said. 'Let's forget it,' but Rattray had followed him by then.

'Where are you off to?'

'I'm fair enough.' He started to walk away, then he turned and he pulled a crumpled pound note from his coat pocket. It was the same one he had tried to give the head waiter.

'Would you do me a favour?'

Rattray was enthusiastic. He seemed to have grown taller as the evening wore on. He was looking down at Jock.

'I'd walk the bloody plank for you.'

Jock blinked. 'That'll not be necessary the night.'

Rattray thought that was funny; he grinned and laughed and repeated it.

'You're a one,' he said.

'A-huh. Will you go to the theatre and pick up Mary Titterington, and give her supper?'

'What, Mary Tits?' Rattray opened his eyes wide. Jock just waited. Rattray said, 'Is she good for it? Eh?' And Jock closed his eyes. His fists closed tight.

'Will you give her supper?'

'Christ I will.' Rattray gave a vigorous nod that was almost a bow.

'You'll find somewhere?'

'Christ, I will.'

'Well, here's a pound to you.'

'I'll no' take your money.' His hackles rose.

'You will. And you'll say I'm sorry. Will you mind that?' Rattray put his head on one side.

'Here, here. Is she expecting you? Is she? She'll no be pleased to see me, eh? Why don't you go along yourself, Jock?'

'I'm asking you.'

'Christ, man!'

'A-huh.' Jock stood still, with the pound in his hand.

'O.K. boy. If that's what you want. Alec Rattray's no the lad to reason why.'

'Good. And you'll mind to say sorry?'

'I will.'

'And you'll get her a good supper?'

'Nothing but the best, Jock.'

'Then here's your money. Now away you go.'

The Orderly Officer was inspecting guard, and Jimmy Cairns was the only one in the Mess when the telephone rang. He was in the billiards room, playing a pointless game of snooker with himself. It was rather cold there, and only the lights over the table were switched on, but once he had begun the game he could not make up his mind to leave it. It was the old story of the bath growing cold. He was too uncomfortable to move. But the Corporal came for him, and he went to the box in the hall to answer.

Two minutes later he was on the telephone to the guard-room, now shivering with an excitement which he was unable to suppress. At last MacKinnon came to the telephone. He knew the voice perfectly well but he double checked.

'MacKinnon?'

'Speaking.'

'This is Jimmy. Look, come back here as quick as you can, laddie. There's been an accident.'

'What's happened?'

Jimmy looked over his shoulder, although there was nobody near. The hall was cold, light and empty.

'Don't let on to anybody. It's serious.'

'Right.'

'I've just had a 'phone call. An officer has been found shot.'

'God. Who?'

'The Colonel,' Jimmy said. 'Now get cracking, laddie.'

Not much longer than half an hour after that, MacKinnon, feeling half excited and half frightened, hurried down the cobbled roads, then branched left over the snow-covered grass in the park. The fog was quite thick in patches, but he could just make out the lights by the old footbridge and he could hear the river running by. All the way across the open ground MacKinnon felt afraid and he kept glancing about him. He tried to force himself to march slowly and he put his hand on the firm leather of his belt, because it gave him courage. But belt or no belt, he was cold with fear when he reached the lamp and he started, as we start when we dream that a seat is withdrawn from under us, when he suddenly observed the dark figure on the bridge. The man was standing with his hands in his coat pockets, staring at the water beneath. He wore a long coat, and he seemed to be frozen there, until suddenly he took a step forward to the parapet, and spontaneously MacKinnon called out, 'Guard!'

When the face was turned to the lamp MacKinnon immediately recognized Jock.

'Who's there?' The voice echoed in the fog.

'Colonel, it's me—MacKinnon.'

MacKinnon had never seen Jock look frightened before. Even when he had replied it still seemed to take Jock a moment to recover himself, then he turned as MacKinnon walked forward. As he recovered he grew more angry, and it was an anger born of fear.

'What the hell are you doing out here at this time?'

Almost guiltily and still looking very pale, MacKinnon drew closer.

'Sir, I was coming across to your house.'

'Are you Orderly Officer?' Jock shouted at him, shouted this question and all the others.

'Yes, sir.'

'Then what the bloody hell are you doing out of barracks?'

'Captain Cairns said, sir . . .'

'I don't care a . . . I don't bloody care what anyone said. D'you know your orders, boy? Do you?'

'Yes, sir.' MacKinnon stood rigidly to attention.

'I'll have you on a charge, d'you hear me?'

'Yes, sir.'

Jock moved forward.

'You've no right out of the barracks gate. You've no right at all. Sneaking about the fields at this time. Did you say you were looking for me?'

'Yes, sir.'

Jock looked at him, but he did not speak for a moment.

His fingers were moving in his pockets but otherwise he held himself quite still.

'The Adjutant sent me, sir. There's been an accident.'

Jock was quiet again. 'A-huh?'

'Colonel Barrow's been found shot, sir. Adjutant got a 'phone call.'

Jock scowled at him. The news did not seem to surprise him. It seemed to have no significance for him at all. Worried by Jock's stillness, MacKinnon continued:

'It's true, sir. Shot himself dead.'

Jock looked at the boy as he might look at a guard coming to take him away.

'Barrow Boy,' he said at last. 'No. You can't be right.'

'Yes, sir. It's true, sir.'

'Aye, it's true. I can see that. I can see fine it's true.' He moved a few steps and pushed the snow with his toe. It was cold that night and damp. Their very bones were cold.

'I shouldn't have lost my temper with you like that.'

MacKinnon did not move.

'If Captain Cairns sent you, you were in your rights.' Then, 'Christ Almighty,' he said wearily. 'Here's a carry-on. Poor Barrow. Poor wee man. Did you ever hear the like?' He gave a funny little shrug and a noise came from him which MacKinnon supposed to be a laugh.

'I'm sorry I surprised you, sir.'

'You didn't surprise me,' Jock snapped.

'Sir.'

Jock looked down at the water. 'Aye, well, and I suppose it had to be somebody,' he said at last.

'Yes, sir.'

'You look like a ghost, laddie. You've a face like a scone.'

MacKinnon still stood to attention.

'Are you feared?'

'Yes, sir.'

'Of the spooks?'

'No, sir. Of you.'

Jock did not laugh at that. He looked hurt and he put his head on one side. 'Of me? You say you're scared of me?'

'I think I should be getting back, sir.'

'No, no.'

'I am Orderly Officer, sir.'

'Jimmy'll take care of that.' Jock waved the objection aside. 'The great James Cairns'll look after that. Aye. He's a great one for fixing things. Who telephoned him anyway?'

'Some farm, sir.'

'Where? Where did it happen?'

'By the bank of the river, sir. So I understand.'

'Aye, by its bonny banks. And only about an hour ago. Is that it?'

'About that, sir.'

'Did you take geography at the school, MacKinnon?'

MacKinnon nodded, but Jock did not care to cross-examine him further.

'This water,' he said sententiously, 'passed him by. It is the same river flowing under our feet. It is the same water.'

MacKinnon nodded even more vigorously.

'Fancy that!' Jock said lightly, suddenly. 'Och, we'll away out of here. It's a lonely place, the bridge, neither one side of the river, nor the other. Why the hell haven't you got your coat on?'

MacKinnon panicked a little.

'I . . . I . . . Haven't I, sir?'

There was an instant as MacKinnon waited for the shout. When Jock really shouted loud a little foam used to form at the very corner of his lips, and MacKinnon suddenly felt he could not bear it. Then the instant passed away, and Jock was not shouting into his face.

He had stepped back and he was chuckling.

'Christ Almighty. I nearly started at you again. Poor laddie. Oh, laddie, don't look like that. Don't look afraid of me. If you knew me better you would not be afraid. Eh? Tell me, what happened to your coat?' He asked quietly and gently, but MacKinnon still did not relax. He looked wary and bewildered.

'In the excitement I forgot it, sir.'

Jock smiled at him kindly. 'That'll never do. Whatever the excitement you've got to remember to eat and keep warm. That's the sign of a soldier. It's only the neurotics that forget to eat. D'you know what a neurotic is?'

'Yes, sir.'

'Maybe Barrow was a neurotic.'

MacKinnon grew braver. 'Not exactly, sir.'

'No. Not exactly. Just bottled up, I suppose. Never bottle up your feelings, laddie. It's against the Queen's Regulations mind, if you don't bottle yourself up. D'you know that? If you want to be a Colonel, laddie, bottle up. I didn't bottle myself up, then I'm no a Colonel. Not the real MacKay. But I'm no drowned in the deep river.'

'Sir.' MacKinnon said.

'You'll come up to the house. You need a dram.'

MacKinnon hesitated. He looked at Jock anxiously with his big faun's eyes.

'Aye, you will come. And you'll no tell them you found me on the bridge. They'll say I've taken to the poetry if they hear that.' He looked hard at the boy. 'You won't say anything about that, will you?'

'Not if you'd rather I didn't.'

'Then you won't.'

'Righto.'

Jock was still standing half towards him and half away.

'How did he do it?' he asked suddenly. 'Did he do it through the head?'

'Through the mouth.'

'Oh.' It was a cry of genuine pity. Jock screwed up his face. 'Mercy me.'

He gave no explanation for the state of the house. There were no fires lit, but every light was burning and every door, including the front door, was open wide. MacKinnon did not like to ask why, and Jock just said, 'Come on round. We'll switch off the lights.'

He closed the front door behind him and he led the way upstairs, where they started to turn off the lights in the bedrooms, to close the cupboard doors and the drawers. All this MacKinnon took, if not for granted, without comment, but when Jock took off his greatcoat and flung it on the bed in his room he could not conceal his surprise. Jock was in full Mess dress. He was in the bright scarlet tunic with gold braid, his best kilt and dress sporran. He was wearing a stiff white shirt and all his medals lay in a single line across his chest. It was an outfit that MacKinnon had never seen worn, although the officers used to wear it for dances and special dinners before the war. There is perhaps no dress so splendid. Jock looked at him, then looked away again to push in a drawer. He said, by way of apology:

'There's a ball at the Welcome. I was in there earlier. Maybe I'm a bit overdressed.'

'It's terrific, sir,' MacKinnon said with wide eyes, and Jock glanced at him in the wardrobe mirror. He was pleased by the effect and he gave a bashful smile.

'D'you think so?'

'I've never seen anything like it. Honestly, sir.'

'Aye. It's an expensive luxury, mind you. And I never get the chance to wear it. The whole thing cost me a couple of hundred pounds, would you credit it?'

MacKinnon gave an open smile, and Jock liked the flattery. He braced back his shoulders and pulled the tunic down so it lay smoothly.

'D'you think it fits?'

'It's perfect. At least I think so, sir.'

'A-huh. Does it suit me?'

'I've never seen you look better, sir.'

'Aye? Is that a fact?'

'Yes, sir.'

'Och, I'm glad of that. I thought I was never going to get the chance to wear it. But I'm glad it's good.'

MacKinnon swallowed. He said, 'You'll get the chance now, sir. Soon we'll be back to full dress. You're the Colonel again now, sir.'

Jock thought for a moment and then he nodded slowly. 'Aye, so I am.' He said, 'C'mon, let's get the place ship-shape. With my daughter away, it gets a wee bit out of hand.' The room was as untidy as it could be. A bomb might have dropped there. Clothes, dirty and clean, dressing-gown, shirts, half the contents of the drawers, were strewn about.

'I'd better fix a corporal from the Mess to come across and look after you in the morning, sir.'

'Aye, that's a good idea.' Jock was surprised by the suggestion. 'You're getting used to the Mess now, aren't you? You never used to open your mouth.'

MacKinnon blushed. 'I suppose I am.'

'It was your grandfather wasn't it, was Colonel?'

'That's right, sir.'

The boy was a far cry from being Colonel, but the link amused Jock. 'A-huh. Are you used to whisky yet?'

'I'm getting used to it, I think.'

'D'you like it?'

'Yes, sir.'

Jock shook his head and laughed. 'Och, c'mon then. Out with the lights. We'll leave this to the Corporal. We'll away down and have a dram.'

MacKinnon took a single to each of his Colonel's double whiskies and they got on very well. Jock had never talked to him before as if he were a man, and MacKinnon grew in confidence.

'There was one thing, sir.'

'Aye, laddie.'

'The Adjutant said to tell you he was awaiting orders about a file of papers the Assistant Adjutant was holding.'

'What's this?' The very word paper made Jock screw up his eyes.

'About a corporal being struck, sir, in a hotel.' MacKinnon looked at him with his big brown eyes, and slowly Jock caught on. Then he began to chuckle.

'It's an ill wind, laddie, that blows no one good. Aye, and they're quick enough, some of these laddies. Jimmy Cairns'll have more in his skull than most of us'll ever guess. That was quick of him. D'you know what it's all about?'

'We all have some idea, I think.'

'The Colonel struck the Corporal, and the Colonel it was that died. . . . You can tell the Adjutant from me that he's to keep these papers in the meantime. He's no to forward them to Brigade.' Jock laughed quite loudly, and MacKinnon, less frightened of him now, began to laugh too. 'I thought they'd gone,' Jock said. 'I thought the report was away. It must have been something that damned fool Rattray said.'

MacKinnon swallowed. He looked hardly more than fifteen, like a midshipman at a pirate's table. He nodded and he said suddenly, 'Yes, Rattray is a damned fool isn't he?'

Jock looked at him astonished. The boy never usually said

boo to a goose. Then he smiled at him. He was genuinely surprised and pleased by him.

'Christ, laddie, the whisky suits you. It does,' and he poured him another. MacKinnon gave a little swagger of his head, and he took a large gulp that burnt all the way down.

'All that bloody Scottish Nationalism,' he said strongly. 'Why, that's tripe and onions.'

'Tripe and onions? Is it? Aye, maybe you're right.' Jock shook his head and he began to laugh again. MacKinnon just smiled broadly at him. Then, looking at the tumbler in his hand, Jock suddenly grew more serious.

'Do I look tired?'

'You look all right, sir.'

'I've never been so tired. I'll never be so tired again, until the day I die. You wouldn't understand it, laddie. But when you've a battalion, and when you've a child, and when you've friends you've fought with . . . Och, I've been carrying it, the whole thing, for five years. And I thought I knew about it. Maybe Barrow knew more than me.' Jock saw MacKinnon frown as he tried to follow, and he smiled.

'I understand, sir,' MacKinnon said. 'Really I do.'

'No. But it's good of you to try. Neither you, laddie, nor anyone else knows just what all these things mean to me. And in one day, in one day,' he looked at the back of his hand, 'with one swipe of the hand the whole thing busts.'

'It must have been a shock, sir.'

'When you get to my state nothing's that shocking. You're kind of punch drunk. You just get more and more numb till there's two of you. And there's one Jock Sinclair knocking about the town with his heart breaking and there's me looking down at him. . . . Laddie, are you scared of me still?'

'No, sir.'

'By reason of the whisky?'

'Not only that, sir.'

'Good for you. I'm sorry I'm no a more cheerful companion. You'll away back to the Mess and say 'Christ, the old boy was weeping in his dram the night'—you will, you will.'

MacKinnon protested that he wouldn't.

'You can trust me *implicitly*,' he said and the expression amused Jock again. He approved of the child.

'I didn't get you right, laddie,' he said suddenly. 'Not right at all.'

MacKinnon did not know what to say. He looked at his cigarette and he said at last.

'I've learnt to smoke properly.'

Jock looked at him, mystified. Then the recollection was clear.

'Christ alive, it was you I shouted at for your smoking, was it?'

'Yes, sir. But you were absolutely right to.'

'Right? To hell with that, laddie. You bloody well smoke as you like. Here, here,' he said and he rummaged in a drawer of the dresser behind him. He fumbled until he found a new packet of cigarettes and he pushed them across the table.

'Here's a packet for you. It's no bloody business of big Jock Sinclair's how you smoke them.'

'Oh no, sir, I couldn't take . . .'

Jock raised his hand. 'You take them. You take them when they're offered.' Then he opened his fingers out and he smiled shyly. 'I want to give them to you, laddie, I want to.'

'Thanks most awfully.'

Jock couldn't get over his expressions.

'"Thanks most awfully." Dammit, dammit,' he said, 'It's a different language altogether.' Then they went on drinking a little longer, and MacKinnon was thrilled by it all. Jock spoke very quietly, and they had talked on many subjects when MacKinnon at last recalled one of the war stories they always told about Jock.

'Is that true, sir?'

Jock nodded. 'It's true enough.'

'But it's fabulous.'

'Did you no hear?' he said with a little smile. 'I'm a fabulous man.' Then when he'd said that the world seemed to fall away from him again and he looked immensely sad, as he remembered. He could see the admiration in the boy's eyes, and for the first time in his life he did not enjoy it. He moved away from the table and stood up. He was suddenly

ashamed. He brushed some ash off his tunic then he turned
and he said:

'You'll no say anything about this get-up, will you?'

'Not if you don't want me to, sir.'

'You will.'

'No, I won't sir.'

'Good for you.'

But Jock was restive now: he was tired of their chat.

'Would your grandad have let his lassie marry a corporal?'

'No, sir.'

Jock clumped his fist down on the table.

'Aye, well I'm going to. D'you hear?'

'Yes, sir.'

'That's what I'm going to do.'

'I'm sure you're right, sir.'

'Och, things'll be fine. I'll fix that, and Jimmy Cairns'll
help fix Riddick and the others. I'll no lie down yet. You'll
see, we'll fix it. We'll forget all the little things. We'll start
anew. D'you know what? D'you know what the real trouble
is?'

'What's that, sir?'

'The Battalion's been at home too long. That's the trouble.
When it's yours, laddie, remember that. There's always trouble when a battalion's too long at home. Remember that.'

'I shouldn't think I'll ever be Colonel, sir.'

'Laddie, d'you want to be?'

'Very much.'

'Then you will be. That's the trick about life. If you want
something bad enough, you can get it. That's the way of
it. Barrow, you know, Barrow wanted to be Colonel. He
told me. He told me this afternoon. Oh, for Christ's sake,
I should have seen it coming. I should have seen it.'

'Oh no, sir. I don't think anybody could have seen it. How
could any one know a thing like that?'

Jock sat down again by the stove and he played with the
poker as he talked.

'You can tell,' he said. 'If you take the trouble to.' He
sighed. 'Och, what a carry-on. D'you know what I said to
him the day when he was trying to speak to me?'

MacKinnon waited.

'I said I wanted to go to sleep. And he just left me. Aye. Och, well. C'mon laddie, it's time you were away back to your chariot.'

But when MacKinnon had gone Jock still walked about the kitchen, smoking cigarettes—'for Christ's sake, like a bloody neurotic.' He sat down and pushed the bottle away. He felt so much that he couldn't feel at all. He was happy that he had been saved. Happy that he should let Morag go, because he already felt the reflection of her smile. He was angry with Charlie, sad about Mary, amused by MacKinnon, annoyed by Rattray, bitterly disappointed by Jimmy, and afraid of what he had let Barrow do. He was all of these things, and none of these things, because he was tired. Exhaustion swept over him, leaving him ragged and apprehensive, too tired to think and too excited to sleep, even now. Worst of all, he knew, as he had known every night since that night in the desert, that in the morning they would be waiting for him to cope with the thing, and suddenly he did not want to cope any longer.

He wanted nothing. It was as if he had prepared himself to die, and death for a joke had passed him by, so that he was doomed to go on making the same noises and meeting the same people, like a ghost of himself. Suddenly afraid, he started to say the Lord's Prayer out loud. But the echo of the very first phrase killed it and he shrugged. He walked over to the shelf and picked out his favourite book. He had put Morag's note to say that she was out with her friend inside the cover of it, when he had picked it up to read it on the previous evening. But now not even the note, not even the lie, seemed to touch him. The book was not the Bible but a book of nursery rhymes which he had practically learnt by heart when he was teaching them to Morag. On the previous evening when he read the little fairy story he had written for her long before, he had nearly cried, but he read it now as if he were looking at it from another world. Even the self-pity had vanished now. It was about a skylark never dying but soaring straight through the golden gates. His eyes passed over the words again and again, but he did not read them. As with the words, so was the rest of the world, and all its

problems. It was like a merciful concussion. The only thing
he could think about now was the riddle that had occurred to
him and he looked at the back of his hand as he said again and
again, 'The Colonel struck the Corporal, and the Battalion
it was that died.' He tried it over again until at last he said
to himself:

> 'The Colonel struck the Corporal,
> And how come that to pass?

'Aye,' he said out loud. 'And that'll finish as a rude
one.' The thought of that gave him just a little relief and
he clenched his fists together.

A colonel does not need an arm to strike with; he needs
teeth to hang on with.

BOOK THREE

The Funeral Orders

The Order Group foregathered in the piping-room, according to instructions. The Regimental Sergeant-Major was there with the Pipe-Major. The Company Commanders were there, and Mr Simpson had unfurled the map over the blackboard. They all stood around, talking nothings, like candidates outside an examination hall. But they stood to attention when Jimmy announced the arrival of the Colonel.

Jock had not looked so smart since the days before the peace. He gave his orders with battle conviction; with complete command; with attack; with effect. They sat in folding cane chairs, silent and attentive as he started according to the book:

'Bonnets off.'

He faced them. He never took his eyes from them. He never referred to a note.

'INFORMATION:

'You see behind me a plan of the streets of the city. Most of the places I mention will be familiar to you but for the benefit of those of you who have confined their outings to a ground sheet on the park there, or a motor run to the nearest country house, I will point out the places to which I refer in the following orders.'

No one laughed at his joke, but nobody was supposed to. He was merely collecting their attention.

He took a deep breath.

'Colonel Barrow was found dead late on the evening of February 20 and on February 23 was adjudged as having committed suicide while the balance of his mind was disturbed. Enquiries were made of his wife, who abides in a London mews . . .'

There was a little stir, and Macmillan nodded as much

as to say he had known. Some pouted and Charlie said out
loud, 'I'd forgotten that one.'

Jock's eyes flashed.

'I do not expect to be interrupted when I'm giving orders.'

The effect was like a slap in the face. Charlie winced.
They all sat up straight in their seats. There was absolute
silence in the room and Jock waited a long time, so that the
effect would sink in. Then, as they expected him to continue the orders he said sharply again, 'Not now; not in the
future; not ever; not by anyone.' And he paused again.
Charlie sat like a statue, with his eyes in front of him.

'Mrs Barrow referred us to her husband's lawyers, Holden
Good and Co. of Bedford Row, London, who stated that the
Commanding Officer had no relations other than his wife.
At her request it was decided that the funeral arrangements
should be made and executed by the officer now commanding
the Battalion.

'The Colonel's remains are at present in the C.R.S. attached
to this barracks. A site for the grave has been found in the
cemetery which lies some third of a mile east of the main
bridge. Here. It lies on the hill.'

Jock pointed on the map with a pointer that had until
then lain untouched on the desk.

'And here.'

He laid down the pointer again and let his hands drop
to his sides. His audience was completely attentive, and
although it was one of those rooms where every scrape of
a chair carries and every cough is magnified, there was still
no sound, but for the echo of the click as the pointer came
to rest on the desk. Jock was breathing faster now. His eyes
moved round the company sitting in the two rows in front of
him. All the other chairs had been folded against the walls
and the floor had been scrubbed for the occasion. Even the
boxes on top of the lockers at the back of the room had been
dusted, and the high narrow windows washed. Jock took off
his bonnet which was tight enough to have marked his brow,
and he smoothed down his hair with his hands, so that it
lay absolutely flat. He looked at them all, and at each one
of them: the Company Commanders in the front and the
Adjutant and Warrant Officers behind.

'All companies, full strength, except for various members of H.Q. Company who will remain in barracks together with the guards and pickets of the day—all companies will take their part in the operation. All officers and other ranks on leave for any reason other than compassionate will be recalled today before 1500 hours. Various officers at present attached War Office and at present attached Royal Military College, Sandhurst, who were personally acquainted with Barrow, will also take part. Regardless of rank or seniority for the purposes of this operation these officers will count as part of this Battalion and the contingent will be under my command.

'The pipes and drums will parade.

'The Burgh police will be acquainted with the orders which follow.

'So much for Information.'

They moved in their seats and Macmillan glanced at Jimmy Cairns and made a little face. The Order Group, like a charger, was held hard at the bit and being pushed on by the urgent boot. It had been the same on the Adjutant's Parade earlier that morning.

'INTENTION:

'The Battalion will bury the Colonel.'

Jock blinked and glowered at Macmillan who gave just the shadow of a smile. He was always inclined to mock the army's more ludicrous regulations. The object of the exercise—to kill the enemy, to capture the castle, or to bury the dead—always struck him as vaguely amusing. Charlie moved his moustache, but he looked quite serious. Jimmy was anxious lest he should miss anything and he had his notebook on his knee. The Pipe-Major nodded at the end of each sentence and the Regimental Sergeant-Major stuck his legs out in front of him, with an air of resistance. Mr Simpson endeavoured to look keen and intelligent and he was so self-conscious that he missed a great deal of what was said.

'METHOD: The Colonel will be given the full honours of the martial funeral.'

Charlie cocked an eyebrow and in reply Macmillan gave the slightest shrug. Jock said 'martial funeral' again, as if in reply to them, then he took another deep breath.

'For the purpose of these orders we can divide the operation into three distinct parts. Before the ceremony. The burial itself. The return to barracks.

'Taking two, first. Exact orders concerning the burial will affect only some senior officers and Warrant Officers and the Padre will run through the service with us tonight at 1930 hours. Parade in the reading room in the Mess.'

The officers were glad to have something definite to write down. Some put '1930, Reading room,' others 'Padre 1930 hrs.' Jimmy Cairns noted all three relevant facts: the time, the place, and the purpose. But as soon as they had made their notes they looked up again. Jock waited until the last word was written down. He did not hurry. Jimmy was biting his lip. The orders were all new to him. Three or four times he had asked Jock what the arrangements were to be, but Jock had ignored him. He had looked straight through him. For two days he had hardly said a word to anybody. He had been building up to this. He still looked nervous, his voice was a little too loud, his gestures a little sudden, but it was a Jock they hardly remembered. The victory and the years that followed had made them all forget the days when he had been nervous and electric like this. Simpson, who had not known him then, was bewildered by the change.

But as the orders continued, and the full scale of the operation was made plain Jimmy grew frightened, and he could see that the others were uneasy too.

It was soon clear that the plan anticipated was the sort of funeral usually reserved for heroes who were also generals. The first picture Jock gave them of the long winding column of men, the music and the mourners, opened their eyes to the scale of the thing. There had not been such a funeral from Campbell Barracks in a hundred years, and there had been a score of colonels since then.

'Before the ceremony:

'The R.S.M. will parade the Battalion in line, A Company on the right, the carrying party and the pipes and drums in the rear, and the colour party, under Mr Simpson, ahead of the line. The extra contingent I mentioned will not parade, but will stand ready by the guardroom under the general guidance of the Quartermaster. They will join the marching column separately in the position which I will indicate in due course.'

He gave some details of the personnel forming the colour and carrying parties, and some orders concerning detailed rehearsals to be carried out that afternoon.

'The carrying party itself will be comprised of the eight senior sergeants acting as bearers and a full platoon of men drawn from all companies to pull the gun carriage.' There was a gasp at that. The gun carriage was reserved for marshals. But Jock continued without pause. 'The whole will be under the immediate command of the R.S.M.'

He moved back, and rolled up the map, displaying the blackboard.

'On my command the Battalion will move to the right in column of threes, and slow march out of barracks in the following order.'

He pointed to the blackboard, and as he read out what was written there he indicated each item with the pointer.

'A Company.

Pipes and Drums.

Carrier Party and Gun carriage.

Colour party.

Commanding Officer, Adjutant, and extra contingent of mourners.

H.Q. Company.

Transport Company, on foot.

B,

C,

D Companies.'

Jimmy at last caught Charlie's eye, but Charlie gave nothing away. Macmillan looked round at Simpson, who was behind his right shoulder, and he made a wry face. Simpson made a schoolboy's gesture with his hands: the sort of gesture boys make when a master is talking about something beyond the class's comprehension. Feet moved, and the chairs creaked a little, while Jock ran on. His voice never varied in tone. The words came loudly and quickly:

'As the Battalion moves off there will be ample time for the various detachments to join at the correct juncture while the companies wheel round the three sides of the square.

The order of march will be final as we pass the guardroom and the barracks gate.

'The R.S.M. will consider the march-off in detail with the several Company Sergeant-Majors and party commanders. I suggest there is a rehearsal parade tomorrow at 1000 hours.'

Mr Riddick always liked to raise an objection, but after the rebuff Charlie had received he was careful to be correct in his behaviour.

'Permission to interrupt, sir.' He stood up, and Jock eyed him warily. He carried the pointer horizontally in his hands.

'Granted,' he said, using his short *a*.

'1000 hours is Battalion Orders, sir.'

'There will be no Battalion Orders tomorrow.' There had been none since the Colonel's death. Jock had had no time for detail, and no inclination for it.

'Begging your pardon, sir, there are several persons under arrest, sir.'

Jock turned back to him, savagely.

'Don't answer me back, Mr Riddick!' He clasped his fingers tightly round the pointer then he moved to the tall desk and he placed the pointer on it softly.

'Not now,' he said, looking down at the desk. 'Not ever.'

Mr Riddick was red and indignant.

He shouted 'Sir' and Mr McLean tapped him on the knee, suggesting he should sit down again.

'My suggestion, perfectly in order,' he murmured indignantly, and Jock looked up at him with pale blue parrot's eyes.

'Ssh,' Mr McLean said, and he leant back in his chair, so it creaked. Mr Riddick felt foolish.

'Pipe-Major!'

Mr McLean jumped. He was afraid Jock had thought he was whispering to Riddick.

'We'll deal with the music after "Intercommunication." I'll come to that later. Understood?'

'Yes, sir. Yes.' His reply was a little song.

'Very well.'

Jock was more like a preacher now. He hung on to the tall desk as if it were a lectern in a pulpit, leaning over it, swaying about it. The sweat was forming on his brow, although all the others in the room were cold. The hands that held the pencils were blue with cold.

'Is the order of march clear, gentlemen?'

Two or three of the officers nodded, and Jimmy mumbled a general assent.

'Clear, Mr Simpson?'

'Yes sir.'

'Clear, Major Hay?' to one of the Company Commanders.

'Quite clear, Colonel.'

'Mr Riddick?'

'Sah.' Mr Riddick still shouted his assent fiercely.

'Very good then.' He unrolled the map of the town again. He took the pointer and stood to one side. The orders were given according to the book.

'The Battalion will proceed at the slow march down to the cross-roads where they will turn right, off Stuart Road.' Always he pointed to the place which he named. 'At this point the band will stop playing and the Battalion will continue along Bridge Road to the High Street.' He followed the whole route, naming in detail every street and every corner and the pointer followed the procession along the map.

'In Lothian Terrace the Battalion will halt and turn by companies and contingents left into line and order arms. The carrier party, colour party, H.Q. group and extra contingent will detach themselves, and they will follow the Padre to the graveside in the following order. They will follow in slow time.

'Padre.

Band contingent.

Carrier party—that is the eight sergeants and the Regimental Sergeant-Major.

Colour party.

Commanding Officer and H.Q. Group.

Mourning Contingent.

Firing party to be drawn from A Company.

'The band party will consist of the Pipe-Major, Corporal-Drummer, and your picked piper. The band remainder will remain . . .'; the noise of the repetition seemed to please him and he began the sentence again. 'The band remainder will remain in Lothian Terrace under the command of the senior sergeant. Mr McLean!'

'Sir?' Mr McLean always sounded anxious to please. His voice was always the very breath of sanity and civility.

'Have you got your pibroch piper picked?'

'Aye, sir. He's waiting next door.'

'We'd better have him in.'

'I'll just be getting him, sir.'

'Obliged.'

The Pipe-Major pushed back his chair and Mr Simpson stood up to let him by. The break was welcomed by everybody and again they all stirred in their seats. Jock himself was lighting a cigarette and there was a little hum of voices. Mr Simpson leant forward to Major Macmillan and he said, 'I'd no idea it was to be as big as this.'

Macmillan raised his eyebrows high. 'I don't think they'd give you or me a show like this.'

But the R.S.M. was more serious in his complaint. He said out aloud:

'Dammit, Montgomery couldn't expect anything more than this.'

Charlie was the only one who spoke up.

'Pretty elaborate do,' he said, but Jock did not seem to hear him. So Cairns followed up.

'How long was Barrow with us, all told?' and he glanced at Jock, but Jock ignored him too. He was preparing the next details in his mind. If he saw that his officers were uncomfortable about the scale of the operation he gave no sign of it. There might have been a soundproof screen between him and the others and his face was quite expressionless until the Pipe-Major returned with the picked piper.

'Corporal Fraser,' the Pipe-Major said, and the Corporal saluted smartly. His face was pale and he still had a dark blue shadow round his eye. Jock was thrown off balance and his hands fumbled for the pointer on the desk. He looked fiercely at the Pipe-Major.

'You didn't say it was Corporal Fraser.'

'No, sir. He's the only one with the pibroch good enough, sir.'

'Aye.'

Jock looked nervously from one face to another, and he tried to recover himself quickly. He pulled himself up and he said, 'The Padre'll give the officers a talk on the ceremony tonight at . . .' He looked blankly at them as he remembered he had said this before. He paused: he looked lost for a moment.

'1930 hours I think, sir.' Jimmy said.

'1930 hours,' Jock echoed, then his eyes wandered back to the Corporal again. He was standing stiffly to attention just inside the door. The blue ring round his right eye made his face look paler, like a moon in the shadows of the corner. For a moment or two Jock seemed to see nothing other than this face. He gazed at it. It was the first time that he had seen the Corporal since he had struck him. All the business of the cancellation of the enquiry had been done through the Pipe-Major. Mr Riddick had not liked it at all: but when he opened his mouth with a threat, Mr McLean looked at him so hard that the words would not come. Charlie, when he learned, just shrugged his shoulders, and said, 'Luck of the game.' Jock nodded, at last.

'A-huh, Corporal Fraser.'

'Sir.'

'I haven't seen you. Where are you staying?'

'Been on a pass, sir. I am back in barracks again now, sir.'

'When did you come back from leave, eh?'

'This morning, sir.'

A little of the old wiliness returned. 'A-huh. Are you married or single, Corporal?'

'Single, sir.'

Jimmy leant forward anxiously. Jock was standing at the side of the little platform by the blackboard, facing the Corporal.

'Colonel, we're short of time. . . .'

'Is Morag with you, Corporal?'

Jimmy had spoken softly and he wondered if he had been heard.

'Colonel . . .'

'Hold your tongue!' Jock glowered down at him. He turned back to the Corporal and spoke softly again.

'Is Morag with you?'

'No, sir.'

'Where is she?'

Charlie shifted in his seat. Major Hay whispered something to his neighbour and the R.S.M. gave a heavy cough.

'One of the officers,' he said, 'should take steps.'

'Wheesht, man,' the Pipe-Major replied.

'Wait, the rest of you,' Jock said without looking at them. 'Answer me, Corporal.'

'She's staying with my people, sir.'

'Where's that?'

'Forres, sir.'

'Christ,' Jock said. 'There's a carry-on. There's a bloody carry-on. At ease, Corporal. Nobody. Nobody told me this. You never told me this, Jimmy.'

'No, sir.' He gave a friendly smile. 'After . . .' he suggested, but Jock waved his hand.

'Och, for Christ's sake: there's no bloody secret now. There have been too many damned secrets and whispers. I like things in the open, and I always have done. That I have. You'll be playing the pipes over the grave, Corporal. Take a seat. We've to deal with the music yet. Sit down like the rest of them and you'll get your orders.'

The Corporal took a chair from the pile at the back, and he brought it up behind the others. He unfolded it and sat down.

'Bonnets off,' Jock said. 'Bonnets off.' And the Corporal put his bonnet on his lap. He had swung his sporran round to his hip.

But Jock could not bring himself back to the orders as quickly as he had anticipated. He was an actor who had forgotten his words. There was a little silence, then he looked at Jimmy and he said fiercely:

'Where the hell was I?'

Jimmy could not recall fast enough.

'Oh, for Christ's sake, someone. Where did we get to? Were none of you listening, eh, is that the way of it?'

Macmillan of all people answered: perhaps his social experience had taught him to keep his head in moments of embarrassment.

'The actual ceremony, I think, Colonel.'

'I told you the actual ceremony's the Padre's business: he'll speak to you tonight at . . . in the Mess at . . .'

'1930 hours, sir.'

'We've been through all that . . .' As he faltered again, Charlie spoke, very calmly.

'Seeing we've come to an interval, I wonder, Colonel . . . This is a pretty elaborate funeral you're planning for, what?'

'Have you an objection, Major Scott?'

'Well,' Charlie poked the point of his crook into a crack between the damp floor-boards. 'It isn't as if Barrow was with us a long time. I mean he may have been a good man and all that but . . . What does anybody else think?'

Charlie leant back as he threw the question open to the others. Jock was standing crouching over the high desk, staring at them.

'Agreed, sir.' Mr Riddick shouted.

'It does seem quite a do,' Macmillan said. Jock waited patiently with a pained smile on his face, and Jimmy spoke again:

'Of course it's right he should get a proper burial, but the whole Battalion, and the gun carriage. Would that not be overdoing it—or d'you not think so?'

He looked back at Jock who made no movement.

All the other Company Commanders, now the tension had been broken a little, said the same thing in different ways and Simpson, because he'd always been taught to speak up, said, 'I mean, the circumstances of his death alone.' And here Jock cut in. He came down heavily on Simpson in his old bullying way.

'The circumstances of his death, eh? What does that mean, Mr Simpson?'

'Well, sir, there's been talk enough. I know it was of unsound mind, but,' his voice trailed away; then as Jock waited he said, 'I mean, sir, suicide's suicide. I'm not sure the Church . . .'

Jock clenched his fists. 'No, it bloody well isn't. It's bloody murder.' With an effort he controlled himself and he threw the next sentence away, so that some of them did not even hear it. 'But that's neither here nor there. For Christ's sake.' He stepped off the platform and he walked over to the window and looked down at the barrack square. Most of the snow had disappeared now, but there was a little pile round the edge of the square. A squad was doubling along from one end to the other under the direction of a corporal with panic in his voice. Jock watched them as if they were toys.

He said, 'I rang his wife, and she had not seen him for three years. I rang his lawyers and they knew of no brothers and sisters. Mind you, he had his friends in Whitehall and he need never have left. Fifteen years after he left this Battalion he came back to it. Fifteen years after he had left Scotland he came back to it.'

He turned his face to them, and he lifted his arms.

'Can you not see?' he asked. 'Can you not understand? And this is the Battalion that's known as the friendly one: and ours is the Mess where it's Christian names only. You mean bastards; you'd grudge him his burial.'

'Oh, hardly,' Charlie said.

'You do, Charlie Scott.'

'It's only the method, Jock.'

'We'll bury him as he should be buried.'

'It isn't as if he even led us in battle.'

'He could have done.'

Charlie's face hardened. 'I merely said he didn't. Jock, whichever way we look at it, we're only burying a colonel.'

'Oh!' Jock shouted it out. 'Oh! Oh, for Christ's sake! Only a colonel. You don't know, do you? None of you; you don't begin to know. Only a colonel! Aye, and that's what he said himself.' He turned back to the window. He seemed now quite out of touch with the others in the room, and he talked as much to himself as to anybody else. He made a little cross in some dust that had formed on the sill: not a Christian cross, but a double cross for noughts and crosses. 'Only a colonel and a colonel's heart. And I wonder about that, too. I'm no sure it's only the Colonel: I'm no sure it isn't the whole bloody glory.'

The murmurs grew louder in the room, and only Corporal Fraser, sitting by himself at the back, kept quiet. He just stared at Jock unbelievingly. Then at last the big shoulders swivelled round and the conversation dried up.

'We'll bury him the way I say we'll bury him, and that's an order, and that's a fact.' He walked quickly back to the platform and he faced them again.

'METHOD:

'After the ceremony. The return to barracks.' He shouted it out loud.

'I say,' Simpson said. 'He's gone round the bend, hasn't he?'

'For Christ's sake, shut up,' Jimmy replied.

'But it's true.'

'Shut up.'

'The groups taking part in the ceremony will slow march back to the formation in Lothian Terrace and the Battalion on my word of command will march off in column of threes, in the reverse order, D Company in advance of the retreat.'

He pointed at the board again, this time with his finger and he went through each group, finishing with A Company.

'When the leading company—D Company in this instance—reaches the crossing of the High Street and Stuart Road the Battalion will halt company by company, contingent by contingent. Then under my general command, but company by company, the column will retreat to the barracks at the slow march. The companies will turn into line, and I will dismiss the parade.'

The last set of orders seemed to take a great deal out of Jock and he leant forward on the desk again, and took a sip of water. The rims of his eyes were pink with weariness. All of the officers, save for Charlie, were staring at him. Charlie was looking at the floor. Like a boxer at the start of another round, Jock moved away from the desk again and stretched himself straight. As he opened the next paragraph, what had been a doubt before now became a terrible certainty. There was an audible gasp, and Jimmy covered his face with his hands. Simpson looked round at the others who looked neither to left nor right. There was no pity in Mr Riddick's eye but he was twitching his little moustache with discomfort. Jock, wide-eyed, rolled into the attack. Nothing would have stopped him now. His face was florid and his eyes were bright. Words flowed from his lips.

'ADMINISTRATION:

'The Colonel will be laid in his coffin in the full scarlet of a Lieutenant-Colonel of this Regiment, his headdress beside him.'

Jock glanced along the line.

'The Adjutant acting with the Q.M. and the Medical Staff will see that this order is discharged.'

He paused and looked at Cairns, who had not moved.

'The Adjutant,' he suddenly said with the voice he usually used for sarcasm, 'is hiding his face. Is my order understood?'

Jimmy did not even want to look at him now. He just glanced up for a second, and he bit his lip. Then he said softly, 'Sir,' And Jock went on, 'The full scarlet. The full dress, even if it has to be tailored tonight. D'you hear me? The full scarlet. Is that understood?'

'Sir.' Jimmy was looking white. He closed his eyes to recover himself.

'The coffin will be carried to the final resting place on the traditional gun carriage which the officer commanding Transport Company will put at the disposal of the Regimental Sergeant-Major commanding the carrying party. Is that understood?'

'Sir.'

'Mr Riddick, is that understood?'

The pantomime continued.

'Understood, sir.'

Soon nobody was looking at Jock; nobody dared, nor did they dare look at each other, any longer. They had turned their eyes away from him much as boys do in a classroom when one of their number begins to cry. Only Mr McLean glanced at him from time to time, and he nodded to show that he was listening. All around him he saw the bowed heads. Not long after Macmillan told some of his friends how ludicrous it had all been: but he was not laughing at the time. He did not feel at all like laughing, at the time. He had the same desire as all the others there, then: he wanted to hide himself.

'The Quartermaster has already been warned about dress. The necessary accoutrements will be drawn from the Battalion stores, company by company, in accordance with the Q.M.'s detail. The aprons and the plaids.

'The full parade rehearsal will be at 1000 hours tomorrow. This afternoon and tomorrow at 0900 hours the separate companies . . .'

There were a score of details, and the orders seemed to go on and on. Jock did not hesitate now. He had remembered the words, but the others still looked away. Jimmy listened and prayed that it would soon come to an end. None of them noted down any of the points: none of them moved. It might have been a stranger standing on the platform, talking so fast. They had a horror of him. Jimmy searched for pity, but could find nothing other than the same horror.

'Mr Riddick will personally supervise the gun carriage drill, and brief the senior sergeants forming the carrying party. Understood?'

'Understood, sir.'

'The Assistant Adjutant will make it his business to report the details of routes and timing to the Chief of Police.'

'Yes sir.'

'INTERCOMMUNICATION:

'The column will be of considerable length and halting by companies or changing time will present difficulty. Warning orders should be passed back from Company Sergeant-Major to Company Sergeant-Major and arrangements for this are again the responsibility of the R.S.M.'

Jock scowled. He seemed to have forgotten something here and he leant forward. The group waited, half expecting him to collapse over the desk, but he pulled himself up again. As the silence continued, the others, one by one, looked up, aware that it was all over. Jock stood perfectly still. He stared down at them until they had all raised their heads, and he completed the formula:

'Any questions?'

Nobody spoke until at last Charlie said, 'Absolutely none.'

Then Jock remembered.

'What about the music?'

'Oh, yes. The music.'

'Aye.' The eyes flared up again. 'There's the question of the music.' They waited with clenched fists.

'Aye, let's see. No music when we parade, but the march off. The slow march. *The Flowers of the Forest*.'

They watched him now. He was talking with feeling again. Every note of the tune seemed to pass through his head when he mentioned the title, and he repeated it. '*The Flowers of the Forest*.' Then he spoke quite plainly as if the recollection just amused him.

'Charlie, you remember that dream I had about Barrow?'

'Sorry?'

'About the Colonel. I had a dream, you mind that day in Mary's house.' The thought of that made him frown. 'In poor Mary's house,' he said, then he brightened up again. 'I said it was a good dream. I told her. And I couldn't mind the dream at all, and you said it must have been a nightmare. I mind it now. The whole Battalion, you see, was lined up on a grey afternoon, lined up ready to move off and at the back there was the gun carriage, with a platoon round it, commanded by a tinker. That's why I'm so sure of the music. We'll have *The Flowers of the Forest* at the ceremony, of course, but we'll have it as we march off too.' He smiled hopelessly and Charlie looked back at him blankly.

'Can't say I remember.'

The smile stayed on Jock's face, but he seemed to have forgotten it. It was a mask.

'In a way, I was right. But I was wrong in thinking it was a good dream. It was a nightmare, after all. You were right about that, Charlie. So you were. Charlie's always right.'

Mr McLean's voice was gentle. 'And after *The Flowers of the Forest*, sir?'

'Aye, we'll have *My Home*, and then it'll be time for the quick ones. The three-fours. What'll be right then?'

'*The Green Hills*.'

'Aye, I like *The Green Hills*. And one or two more but most of the way through the town you'll no play. Play when you turn up the hill there.'

'Sir.'

Jock was warm again:

'The Burial Party. Your one corporal'll lead with the traditional *Flowers of the Forest* there again, the whole way from the gates to the grave, and take it slow, Pipe-Major, take it slow.'

'Yes, sir.'

'Now what about the pibroch?'

'That's for the Corporal, sir.'

Jock looked over their heads at the Corporal, who nodded. Jock winced when he looked at the bruise on his face and he lifted his own hand to his eye.

'Are you right?' he asked. 'You're all right?'

'I'm all right, sir.'

Jock blinked. 'I'm glad of that. I'm glad of that. So you'll choose your own pibroch.'

'Sir.'

'And what'll it be?'

'*Morag*, sir.'

'*Morag*, aye. Can you manage it?'

'Aye, sir.'

'You're a man after my heart, Corporal. That's the bloody silly thing.' Then he turned back to the Pipe-Major.

'The death they say is a victory. The death they say's the great triumph. We'll march away to the *Black Bear*. The *Black Bear*'s to pull us together.' Jock was lost in the music again. 'Then the regimental march; *Scotland the Brave*; the *Cameron Men*; some others, Pipe-Major?'

'*The Cock o' the North*.'

He was suddenly angry, like a turkey: 'Yon's a cheesy tune. You'll no play that till Charlie Scott here's Colonel. You'll no play that. Some others, aye. *Lawson's Men*'d do.'

He tapped his fingers on the desk and he mentioned several more marches.

'All the tunes of glory!' he suddenly cried. 'We'll have them all, to remember the more clearly. We'll have all the tunes of glory!' He turned towards the window again and he raised his hands with a triumph and excitement: he stared up at the sky and his eyes glistened as he said:

'It'll be a right funeral. I know it will. It's as I said. I've seen it once already. And it'll be the least we can do.' He wheeled round again, and the moon faces watched him.

'And all along Stuart Road, Mr McLean, along Stuart Road until the cross-roads . . .' Suddenly he looked back at the window again and he said very quickly with a sort of clown-like bathos, 'We'll have no music at all: all along the road there, we'll have no music. Just the long column winding through the town, winding all the way. Just the noise of the marching and the straps and bayonets. Just the rattle of the wheels of the empty gun carriage, bumping along the cobbles there. And all the people'll be watching us. Mr Riddick, the marching must be perfect. D'you hear me? Perfect!'

It had gone too far again for anybody to stop him: there was no chance of interruption now, and again the heads began to drop. But this time Jimmy did not lower his eyes. He watched Jock all the time, with awful anguish, as he talked on and on. It was as if he could not leave off: as if he knew that it was his last speech in court, and when that was ended, all was ended. With a fever, with every gesture, his voice growing loud one moment and soft the next, he went on and on.

'. . . And it'll snow again. Those are the snow clouds there. But the snow'll not break until the end of the day. It'll not start snowing until the parade is over. When we're finished it'll snow. But when we march back from the hill it'll be bitter cold, and a wee bit misty maybe, and pink, over the roofs. I see it fine, with the aprons over the kilts and the pink picked out in the stone of the houses: and the daft purple of the drapes over the kettledrums. Now the last bit . . .

'Aye, the last bit. The last bit into the barracks at the slow march. We'll no have the *Flowers* then, nor any other tune.' He suddenly spotted Charlie and he said quickly, 'We'll no have *Charlie is my darling*, either.'

He turned his head in a little circle and he spoke softly, almost secretively as he walked back to look at the barrack square below. 'We'll not have the pipes at all. That's how we'll do it. We'll come the last bit through the gates with the muffled kettledrums alone. No music at all. Just the drums. The whole long column, the whole Battalion of us at the slow march and just the four kettledrums rapping, beating, with a die—with a *die, dittit-die, dittit-die.*'

He waited, and there was no sound. He turned very slowly and his face was frozen with a curiously questioning expression. The tears were pouring down his cheeks. For a terrible moment he must have seen himself reflected in their eyes.

Slowly he put his hand to his face and felt the wetness of the tears. He looked about him, trapped and appalled, then again he was quite lost and he moved like a waif across the room.

There was silence until Mr McLean's voice broke gently, like a soft wave on an Atlantic shore.

'Aye, sir,' he said, 'it will be done exactly as you have said.'

Jock did not turn back to them, so Mr McLean got up without another word, and the others followed. They walked from the room leaving only Charlie and Jimmy behind, and when they were outside they dispersed immediately, going their different ways in silence, like monks.

Inside the room Charlie moved slowly towards his friend as if he were approaching an animal and he said, as he always said:

'Jock, old chum' and Jimmy said, 'Laddie.'

It was then that he broke. It was then with a great groan of relief as much as of sorrow that it came to an end for him. It was the end of what had started in a desert. His shoulders began to shake, his lip quivered and first he gave a whimper. Then with great gulps of air like an inconsolable child, he began to sob while the two officers supported him.

'All right, laddie; all right.'

'We'll tell Mary,' Jimmy suggested kindly but Jock shook his head violently. They got a car and put him into it because he asked, at last, to be taken home.

'Tell Morag, you fools, tell Morag, and take me home.' And there were soldiers passing by, who stared at him. 'For Christ's sake,' he said. 'I'm bashed the now. Oh, my babies, take me home!'